The Demise of Garsuna:

Book 1

Jason of Joebanya

Copyright © 2024 J.P. Jarvis
All rights reserved. ISBN: 979-8-89324-118-1
Printed in the United States of America.

No part of this publication shall be reproduced, transmitted, or sold in whole or in part in any form without the prior written consent of the author, except as provided by the United States of America copyright law. Any unauthorized usage of the text without express written permission of the publisher is a violation of the author's copyright and is illegal and punishable by law. All trademarks and registered trademarks appearing in this guide are the property of their respective owners.

The opinions expressed by the Author are not necessarily those held by the Publishers.

The information contained within this book is strictly for informational purposes. The material may include information, products, or services by third parties. As such, the Author and Publisher do not assume responsibility or liability for any third-party material or opinions. The publisher is not responsible for websites (or their content) that are not owned by the publisher. Readers are advised to do their own due diligence when it comes to making decisions.

I would like to thank my parents, Jeff and Kerry, for their unwavering support.

And a huge thanks to Ian Mulhern, for all the pointers and discussions that bolstered the content of my writing.

About the Author

As an Ohio native, Jacob spends much of his time daydreaming of places much more fantastical than his backyard. Whether that's from the mystical worlds of Greek Mythology from the West or the diverse ecologies of Manga from the East.

When forced to be tethered to the real world, Jacob immerses himself in the beauty of nature, exploring the driest of deserts to the snowiest of mountains.

Educated in Psychology and Human Behavior, Jacob is most interested in understanding why we do what we do and how we humans fit in this chaotic world we call reality.

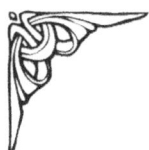

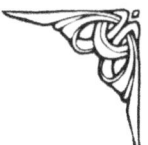

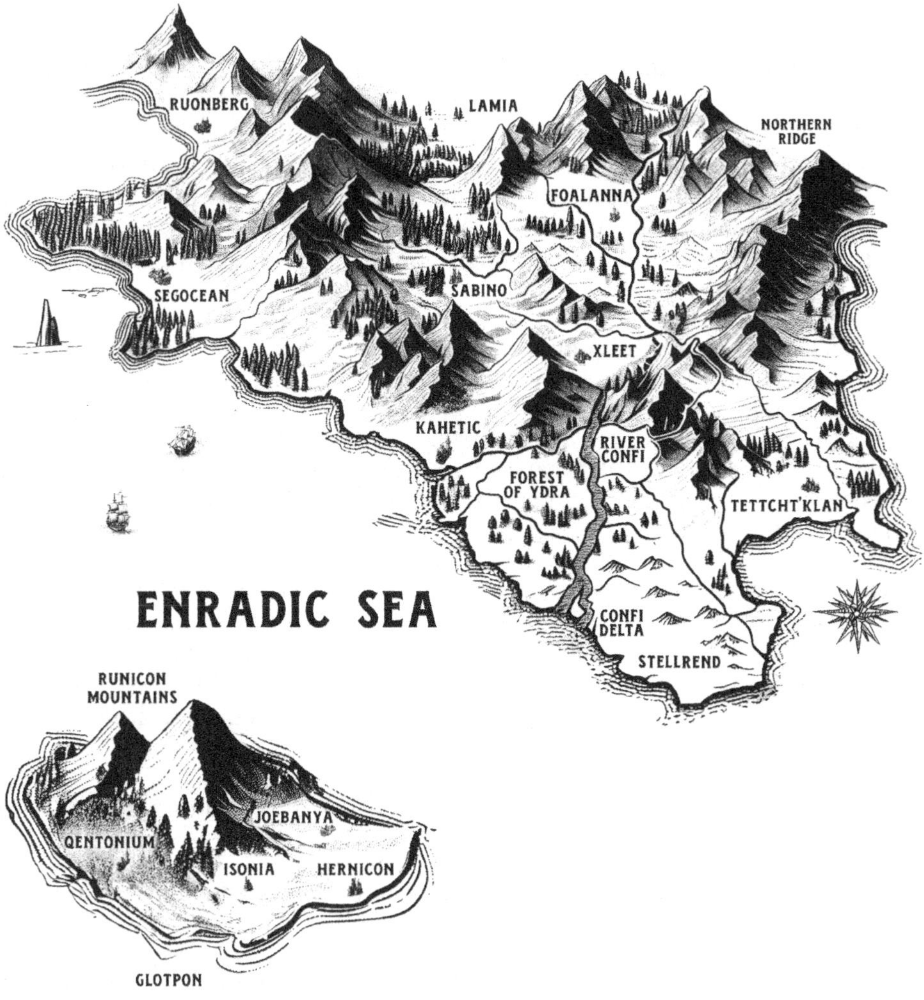
RUONBERG
LAMIA
NORTHERN RIDGE
FOALANNA
SEGOCEAN
SABINO
XLEET
KAHETIC
RIVER CONFI
FOREST OF YDRA
TETTCHT'KLAN
ENRADIC SEA
CONFI DELTA
STELLREND
RUNICON MOUNTAINS
JOEBANYA
QENTONIUM
ISONIA
HERNICON
GLOTPON

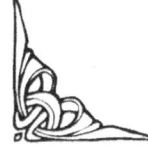

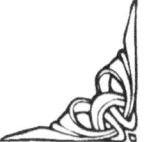

Chapter 1
Jason

Tink. Tink. The distinct rhythm of metal smacking metal rang out across the deserted streets of Joebanya. The noise was faint at first, originating from deep within the Great Furnace near the center of the city. Tink. Tink. Then, just as the first sun rose over the Runicon Mountains, the sound spread like wildfire. Tink! Tink! Like a heartbeat, the rhythm brought life to the city of Crafters. While the symphony of metalwork committed subterfuge on the silence of morning above ground, there was a completely different commotion coming from beneath the surface.

"Busters, you're up!" The command was barked by a bald man who stood with a group of miners at the mouth of a newly formed cave. Though, at this point, it was less of a cave and more of a dent in the mountain.

Four scrawny teenagers and one heavy-set man, who was as large as all four of the teenagers combined, stepped forward and proceeded into the crevice. As they disappeared into the mouth of the cave, the Commander called out, "Ready?!"

Jason, one of the scrawny teenagers, outstretched his arms as he entered the cave. It wasn't long until his palms contacted the cold stone wall. Just as he was trained, Jason created an A-frame with his legs by planting his right foot firmly into the corner of the stone wall and the debris-laden floor. Then, the fifteen-year-old bent his elbows into a ninety-degree angle with the wall, and it looked as if the team of Busters was going to open up the cave by pushing down its walls.

"Ready!" Jason and the four others exclaimed asynchronously as they each found their position.

"Steady!" The Commander responded, cautiously inching further from the mouth of the cave.

Jason dug in his heels as he took a deep, steady breath through his nose. He had done this a hundred times before; nothing to be worried about. Earlier was just a fluke, a mistake. Everyone makes those. Jason tried to expel his worries with a long exhale through his mouth, but it did little to lessen the tightness in his chest.

"Ruo of the Rejuvenating Flame…" It was Erik, the man amongst the Busters, who initiated the chant.

Jason and the other teenagers echoed Erik with chilling solidarity, "Ruo of the Rejuvenating Flame…"

"Bestow onto me the same blessing you bestowed upon my ancestors…" Erik continued.

"Bestow onto me the same blessing you bestowed upon my ancestors…" the four other Busters mimicked.

"So that I may see the impure…"

"So that I may see the impure…"

As Jason recited the prayer, he focused on the warmth that radiated from deep within his chest, trying to suppress as much of that energy as he could.

"And have the strength to remove it," Erik said without missing a beat.

"And have the strength to remove it."

"A'Stavi." Erik finished the chant.

Jason braced himself as he and the others concluded with a hearty "Gilaheed."

"FIRE!!" As Erik uttered the order, a look of wicked bewilderment filled his eyes as if he just ordered the genocide of all geology. But that wild look, a look of pure, primal joy, was quickly replaced by gawking confusion as the cave was illuminated in a blindingly bright light. Then, Erik and his four subordinates were launched off their feet and sent flying backward.

Luckily, there was a coalition of miners waiting outside to break their fall. Otherwise, Erik, Jason, and the rest of the Busters would've tumbled five-thousand feet down the barren side of the Runicon Mountains. The company of miners hurriedly helped the Busters to their feet, except they didn't help Jason. The Commander slowly strutted from the back of the group to the front, his hands neatly crossed behind his back.

Jason rolled onto his stomach and tried to push himself to his feet. His arms proved too weak, and he fell flat on his face.

"What's happening to me?" Jason thought to himself ruefully.

"On your feet, boy." It was the Commander, who now hovered over Jason like a vulture.

Erik grabbed Jason by his slim shoulders and effortlessly hoisted him to his feet. Jason could now see that the entire company of miners had formed a circle around where he and the Commander stood.

"Sir!" Jason bowed as deeply as he could, trying to hide his face.

The other miners had already started their jeering. "Worthless mut," "purple-eyed freak," "who does this guy think he is?" "reckless," "nobody."

The Commander placed two fingers on Jason's chin and forced their eyes to meet. "I know it was you."

"I'm sorrr…" but that's all Jason could get out.

"This is the last straw." The Commander spat on the stony surface of the mountain, but it might as well have been directly in Jason's face. "You're not practicing with the priests anymore, boy; this is the real world. I will not have some showoff putting the rest of my company in danger!"

"I'm not trying to…" the Commander dropped Jason's chin, and the boy bit his tongue.

"You're done," was all the Commander said before turning his back. "Alright, Sweepers, get this rubble cleared out! We don't have all day!"

Jason straightened out of his bow and looked towards his fellow Busters. None of them returned the gesture. Jason conceded and started for the trail that would take him down and around the mountain into the city of Joebanya below. He was able to suppress his tears for most of the walk home.

Chapter 2
King Akinish

There were very few people, if any, on the entire island of Glotpon who held as much influence as King Akinish, the King of Isonia. The House of Akinish has maintained peace amongst the four provinces of Glotpon (Joebanya, Isonia, Qentonium, and Hernicon) for more than three hundred years. A feat that no other nation in the entirety of Garsuna could claim. But that was all about to change.

King Akinish stood at the center of the Temple of Isaa, accompanied by his son, Prince Akinish, and the High Priest of Isonia, Casaba. The massive, monolithic marble walls that surrounded the men made them seem no more significant than ants as they faced the open entrance of the temple. Behind the men, set on a stage, was a gilded statue of Isaa, the God of Water. The God was depicted wielding a harpoon in one hand and an oar in the other. Aside from a sash that was draped across Isaa's body, the rest of the statue of the God was naked.

The trio appeared to be waiting for someone to join them as they stared intently towards the temple's entrance. After several silent minutes, something finally slipped through the door's threshold. It was a beam of light that shone as the setting of the first sun intersected perfectly with the frame of the temple's entrance.

"The last days of the wet season are upon us." King Akinish sighed and shook his head, sending a flurry of dancing lights along the temple's interior as the sunlight shone off the King's jeweled crown. "We must prepare for the coming of the harvest."

King Akinish spun in a half circle, putting his back to the entrance and his front to the statue of Isaa. The sunlight had set the gilded statue ablaze, creating a certain radiance within the God's figure that seemed to bring the statue to life. A cold, derisive bitterness ran through Akinish as he realized he hadn't seen the statue laminated in the light of both suns since he took his father's spot on the throne. It would be at least another hour before the second sun got low enough. The King spun around once more, this time with enough vigor that his royal red robes flew up on his sides. The High Priest was fast on Akinish's heels as the King made for the exit.

"King Akinish!"

"What is it, Casaba?" The King looked sidelong at the High Priest with his pale purple eyes but otherwise held his stride.

"There has been a sign, my Lord. An omen that should not be ignored."

"I haven't got much time," King Akinish started to say as he nodded glibly toward a couple of Isonians who passed. "I am to leave for Qentonium at once. But please, do fill me in."

"Just this morning, I saw an eagle soaring over Isonia, a serpent tight in its talons."

"Was the serpent dead or alive?"

"It thrashed so vigorously, I thought it'd free itself and fall from the sky."

"So, deceit makes its way into my city…"

"There is only one reason that the Gods would send such a sign. Our enemy is soon to make…"

"I will certainly keep that in mind, Casaba." The King stated firmly, shooting another sideways glance at the High Priest. "Thank you."

The pair walked in silence until they reached Akinish's palace, located a short distance from the Temple of Isaa. Two of Akinish's Delegates stood, waiting at attention, within the palace's front courtyard. King Akinish ordered them to go to the stables on the outskirts of Isonia and ready his carriage. The Delegates bowed before scurrying off to complete their task.

"My Lord…" The King stopped for the first time since leaving the Temple of Isaa and turned to face Casaba. "Your people have been cut off from the rest of Garsuna for so long, but I fear that will not always be the case. My being here is proof enough of that. Please, I implore you, you must prepare your people."

"The Gods sent you here," Akinish said flatly. "Blown off course, just as my ancestors were. Glotpon cannot be reached intentionally, and there is no vessel that can make the voyage. We've been through this, Casaba."

"The Segoceans have built such a vessel, my King. One that can survive the Enradic Sea with a legion on her back. I have seen it."

"Then Isaa will raise the waves to meet this newly made vessel." The King prepared to pivot away from the conversation once and for all. But Akinish's escape was thwarted when Casaba snatched his wrist, and the King's face flushed redder than his royal robes.

"You should never underestimate the ability of man. Alone, they are nothing. But when they work together, man can achieve what even the Gods thought impossible."

"Yes, teacher," Akinish submissively replied as he tried to free himself from the High Priest's grip.

"You WILL unify your people, and you WILL prepare them for war. Because if you don't, you will kill us all."

"Yes, teacher," King Akinish said, finally pulling himself free from the High Priest. The King scanned his empty courtyard as he awkwardly straightened his robes, ensuring the pair was alone. "What would you have me do?"

Casaba produced a ghastly grin, revealing several gaps present amidst the aging man's teeth. "That will be the easy part."

CHAPTER 3
Jason

By the time Jason finished walking home, the second sun was at high noon, marking the middle of the day. Jason lived with his parents in an average abode for a Joebani commoner. Their home was dug into the dirt and consisted of three rooms. A main room where the family prepared food and ate, and two bedrooms. The bedrooms were set parallel to one another and were separated from the main room by a removable wooden partition.

"Hey, hun, you're home early," it was Jason's mom, who sat bent over a piece of slate rock. The rock acted as a table, holding small metal beads, which Jason's mom strung along a thin metal twine. Their family will use this jewelry later to barter for fish and vegetables.

"Yeah," Jason tersely said as he moved in to embrace his mother, who stood to greet him.

"What happened?" Jason pulled away from the embrace and sat, crisscrossing his legs, on the dusty floor.

"I... I really don't know." Jason stared intently into an indistinct spot on the floor, looking for an answer that wouldn't cause any worry in his mother. "The Commander said I was done after the second bust of the day."

Jason's mom positioned herself to sit directly across from her son. "It isn't your fault." Jason nodded silently. "No, Jason. It isn't."

Jason lifted his head to meet his mother's eyes. She was the only one who didn't immediately pull away from Jason when she saw his dark purple eyes, and it opened him up like a cracked nut. "It is my fault! It's because I don't know how to control my blessing! I can't even keep a job as a Buster, the easiest position a Miner can have! I'm more useless than that oaf Erik, so what does that make me, then? Nothing but a purple-eyed freak..." Jason's eyes returned to the floor.

"You can't listen to what those other men say about you. They see your Isonian eyes and immediately explode with envy. Besides, you're due for your second blessing at the next End of the Month Service." Jason's mom lightly placed a hand on his shoulder. "Everyone starts to struggle with their blessing at your age. That's why King Akinish grants us another when we're adults." Jason looked up to find his mother still staring at him with her large, dark brown eyes that matched her swarthy skin. "Come on, help me grab some water before your dad gets home, or it'll be both our butts."

The water tank was located on the southside of Joebanya, fed by an aqueduct from the fresh water springs of Isonia. It wasn't too far of a walk from Jason's home and he was happy to have something to keep his mind off his problems, even if just momentarily. His mom always knew how to turn a bad day into an alright one. When they got back from the tank, Jason's mom poured some of the water into a pot and set it over the firepit. Then she placed one of her hands on the wood pile, sparking a fire immediately. That is when Jason's dad got home.

Jason's father didn't even acknowledge his existence on the way in. Instead, he stumbled across the house's main room and nearly fell into the fire, trying to get to Jason's mom. She quickly kissed him on the cheek before tossing a piece of overly salted fish into the boiling water.

"Heard what you did this morning, boy," Jason's father said reproachfully. "Damnit, near all Joebanya is talking about it. You do know what a Buster is supposed to do, don't you?"

"Yessir."

"Then why'd you try and blow up the entire damned mountain!?" Jason's father stomped furiously, sending dust in every direction. "You know how embarrassing that is for us!? Our child has no self-control. He's just like every other Isonian-born piece of..."

"It's fine, really," Jason's mom interjected. "He'll do better next time, right..."

Jason's father thrust a vindictive finger into his wife's face. "Stay out of this, woman. It was your sister who got us into this mess. So far as I'm concerned, this is all your fault." Jason's mother mimicked her adopted son and looked to the floor. "I've decided. Jason, you're fifteen now; it's time for you to grow up. So, tonight is your last night under my roof."

"Yessir." Jason glanced at his mother, who kept her eyes glued to the floor.

"How much longer 'til dinner? I'm starving." Jason's father sat down on the dusty floor and warmed his hands over the open fire. He didn't say so much as another word to Jason for the rest of his life...

CHAPTER 4
Jason

With each day that passed, Jason tried to remind himself that he was one more day closer to getting his second blessing. He tried to go back to work, but the Commander refused his entry. He even went to the Crafter's Union to find work under a different Commander, but the same issue arose. Every time Jason tried to use the powers entrusted to him through Joeb's Blessing, he went completely overboard, threatening to collapse the cave. The last Commander sent Jason home with a warning, "the next time you come onto a site and try to recklessly bust rock, you'll be blacklisted from the Union!"

Jason went to the only place he could think of where he'd be welcome without any gold or silver. The Temple of Joeb. Jason walked in to find several other miserable souls, drunkards and unlucky gamblers, in the same shape he was. As Jason approached, the knaves saw his dark purple eyes and turned their backs, so he found a seat in the pews on the opposite side of the Temple.

One of the four priests who sat at the front of the Temple, kneeling towards the gilded statue of Joeb, noticed Jason as he entered. The priest quickly disappeared into a side room and reappeared with several slices of bread and a bowl of room-temperature stew. As the priest approached, Jason couldn't help being slightly amused by how the distinctly orangish brown color of the priestly robes blended with the wooden furniture of the Temple. In the dim torchlight, the priest almost looked to be nothing more than a floating head.

"Welcome to the Temple of Joeb, Craftsman of the Gods. Are you here on behalf of King Akinish?"

"No, I am not," Jason looked away.

"Oh, I'm sorry, I just thought because of your eyes…" The priest was silent for a while, and Jason started to eat. The bread was stale, so the only palatable way to eat the combo was to dip the bread into the stew. But that was alright with Jason, for it was the only thing he had to eat all day. "So what DOES bring you to the Temple of Joeb, then?"

Jason looked sidelong at the priest between bites. He knew they were only extending him a courtesy, doing their priestly duty. "I don't have anywhere else to go." That was all he said.

The priest looked at him quizzically as if they didn't trust that answer. As they made to leave, the priest called out curtly, "the Temple of Joeb will accept any in need!"

After the cold stew and old bread, Jason tried laying down along one of the wooden pews. The band of bums maintained a consistent mumble that made it hard to find sleep, and a pang of jealousy rose in Jason, one that he was all too familiar with. He wished that he could join those degenerates. Laugh with them, smile with them, even be angry with them. But not even they would have him.

Unable to sleep, Jason sat up and looked straight ahead at the gilded statue of Joeb. Dressed in only a Victor's Sash, as all Gods and Goddesses are depicted, the Craftsman of the Gods clenched a chisel in one of his seven-fingered hands and a square in the other. All the Gods have an attribute that sets them apart from their Descendants, and Joeb's was having extra digits.

Jason knelt, putting his knees on the dirt floor and resting his forehead on the back of the bench in front of him. "Joeb of the Chisel, Joeb of the Furnace, and Joeb of the Craft. Lend me your fire so that I may light my way forward. Lend me your chisel so that I may carve the best path for myself. And lend me your knowledge so that I may be of use to my people. A'Stavi, Gilaheed." Jason spent the rest of the night desperately pleading with Joeb for direction, but he received no response.

CHAPTER 5
Catrina

Qentonium is the largest of the four Provinces of Glotpon, at least by land mass. As far as population density, it is the second smallest (only larger than Isonia). That is because Qentonium is the agricultural center of the island country, composed of massive plantations. Each plantation is managed by a sole family, appointed by The Council, which is the governing body of each respective Province. The farmhands and ranchers who worked on Qentonium's plantations were auxiliary parts of the family that were appointed by the Council, either cousins or in-laws.

"Is it true..." Catrina started as she picked through her breakfast of boiled vegetables. "Is it true that King Akinish is back already?" Catrina sat at an elegant, extended table with her family of seven.

"Aye, it is true," Catrina's father, Traxione, started to say. "This has been the shortest wet season that I can remember. I hope we can scrounge up enough food to last the coming dry season. You know what they say, the shorter the wet, the longer the dry."

"What if there isn't enough?" Catrina asked as a lock of blonde hair fell in front of her emerald eyes, both traits she shared with her father. Traxione smiled at his daughter, but it was his wife who responded.

"Then some of the scoundrels will starve, nothing you need to worry about deary. Right Traxione?" Catrina set her silverware down with a faint clamor.

"Well, if we don't harvest enough for everyone, I offer all my extra rations."

"She gets more and more like her mother with each passing day, doesn't she?" Catrina's step mom asked rhetorically, with a smirk.

"It makes me so proud," Traxione said with a faint smile. Catrina put her hands in her lap. The crimsoness of her embarrassment exaggerated the young woman's already defined facial features.

"With King Akinish's arrival, that means in one month's time, after the harvest has concluded, it will be time for the Festival of Mahon." Traxione skillfully steered the conversation back on track.

"Have you decided where I will be spending the Festival, father?" Catrina looked to Traxtione like all daughters do when they wanted something.

"I am sorry, Kick," Traxtione averted his gaze from Catrina's doll eyes. "We cannot afford to lose the favor of the Council. They're already upset that I have yet to produce a legitimate heir. They've threatened 'restructuring' if another win isn't secured at Mahon's Festival. That is why I must send my most venerated daughter!"

"But father, I could produce our family an heir, a son…" Catrina's step mother's eyes stabbed her all over. "And Carey became eligible this year…"

"That is true. But Carey does not have the experience that you do… Tell you what, bring home Qentonium's fourth consecutive victory, and I promise I will find you a suitable husband."

Catrina beamed and then bowed. "Yes, father!"

Traxtione kept his attention on his eldest daughter, a look of regret in his eyes. "If only you were born a boy…" he said softly. Catrina knew her father meant that endearingly, but she still hated to hear it, and she finished her breakfast in silence.

After helping her stepmom with cleaning the silverware and plates, Catrina went out into the fields to practice with her blessing. It had been since the last Festival of Mahon that she even needed to use it. Truthfully, Catrina thought that by this time, she'd already be making plans for her own family, like every other nineteen-year-old woman. Qentin's Blessing should've been nothing but a fond memory. "Father knows best," she reminded herself. "Just one more year, be patient."

It took a while for Catrina to find a spot to practice, as she didn't want to damage any of the crops this close to harvest. The Qentonians were meticulous when it came to using their land, and due to Garsuna's two suns, the flora received excessive energy, allowing for plant growth in immense proportions. Eventually, Catrina found a patch of bare soil in the shade of an outstretched oak.

Catrina positioned her body into the shape of a T underneath the oak, legs together and arms placed perfectly perpendicular to her torso. She wiggled her toes, focusing on the warmth of the soil on her bare feet. Catrina envisioned her legs as the roots of a tree, taking the soil's warmth and spreading it throughout her body until it reached the tips of her fingers.

"Qentin of the Trees, Originator and Propagator of plants. I ask for the same guidance you gave your daughter, Mahon," as Catrina recited the prayer, her emerald eyes began to emit a soft, emerald light. "Help me to understand the language of the leaves so that I may hear their wants and their needs. So that I may properly spread their seeds."

Slowly, two beautiful baby oaks sprouted underneath Catrina's open palms, and she grinned at her success. "Still got it," she thought. After springing up several more oaks, Catrina rushed back home.

CHAPTER 6
Jason

Jason had fallen asleep, mid-prayer, with his forehead firmly planted on the bench's back support. He awoke to find that the vagabonds, who were on the opposite side of the Temple, had been replaced by Joebani citizens. The Temple of Joeb was beginning to fill for the End of the Month Service, which occurs every forty-three days. All the citizens of Glotpon observe the last day of the month as a sacred day of rest, as Garsuna would rest during the formation of the world. As such, they are expected to start the day at the Temple of their Pronvince's patron God. This was also the time that any newborn citizen, or ones who had recently reached adulthood, would receive their blessings.

Standing at either side of the Temple's entrance were two Delegates from Isonia. They greeted the citizens as they entered by name and jotted down whoever was in attendance on a long scroll. They wore lavish, purple robes that increased the intensity of their pale purple eyes. Unlike Jason's muddied eyes, the Delegate's eyes were so light they were nearly pink. Tethered to the Isonians' backs, they wore perfectly square leather satchels. Jason knew that inside each satchel was one of Joeb's God Tools.

Jason vacated his spot amongst the wooden benches and went to lean against the Temple's massive stone walls. This is where he normally went for End of the Month Services, and he hoped his mom would know where to find him.

It wasn't long until the Temple of Joeb was teeming with people. The crude commotion contaminated Jason's conscience, creating a fleeting sense of claustrophobia, and he began tapping his thumb against his thigh. That is when the three members of Joebanya's Council took the stage, standing directly in front of the gilded statue of Joeb. Jason knew they were members of the Council from their pristinely white robes, a rarity if not a Kigulbisisian impossibility as a working member of Joebani society. The crowd reduced their ruckus until the only noises Jason could hear were the crackling of lit torches and the melody of the morning's birdsongs.

"Thank you all for being here on time. We will wait for the rise of the second sun to start the Service, as is custom," one of the Councilmen announced. "That being said, the Council has some issues they would like me to address. So we don't eat up ALL the time of Garsuna's Rest. We shall do that now." Several of the older members in the crowd gruffed their disagreement. "Many of you may be aware that we plan to open up the quarry again for the dry season. This will be a great opportunity for new jobs, as well as give some of our youth a wider breadth of experiences. But, we cannot ensure these jobs until we have the parcels necessary to expand the Temple of Joeb. If you own land in the area surrounding the Temple, please come see me at the end of today's Service. We are paying double the gold you bought the land for, and we'll relocate you to a nicer lot free of charge! Remember, Tette is fickle with her fortunes, so roll the dice now while we're still asking! Secondly, for those of you who have children who want to participate in the Festival of Mahon, we will be taking donations starting today. Lastly, A'Stavi!"

The "Gilaheed" response was weak, but it acted as a spark that scorched the entire Temple with sound. Young men complained to their fathers to sell their family land, while old men complained to their sons about learning to respect their inheritance. "It must be nice to share things within a family," Jason thought. "Why are they getting so upset with each other?"

Several minutes passed, but it did nothing to pacify the problem perpetrated by the Councilman. When the High Priest of Joebanya, evident by her black robes, stepped up to the stage with her lesser priests, she rose one hand high above her head. Like a lever, the lower the High Priest dropped her hand, the quieter the crowd got. Until silence once again found the Temple.

"Welcome, welcome, Brothers and Sisters, children of Joeb. They who are the most skilled craftsman and miners in all of Garsuna, A'Stavi!"

"Gilaheed!" The response was hearty, unlike the crowd's response to the Councilman.

"Isonia has sent word that the end of the wet season draws near, bringing the wickedness of the dry season. But in Joebanya, our jobs aren't dictated by the coming and goings of the rain. Neigh, here in Joebanya, we push through the dry season unabated! A'Stavi!"

"Gilaheed!" The response was thunderous, and several of the citizens thrust their fists over their heads.

"But that does not mean we charge through the dry season like a blind brava bull. One must be reserved, rational, resourceful, and, above all else, selfless. Look after your friends and family, and each and every one of us will live to see another wet season, A'Stavi!"

"Gilaheed!"

"As a reminder, at the next End of the Month Service, we will be picking fifteen individuals to participate in the Festival of Mahon. Only those who have received their second blessing and who do not yet have a spouse may enter. We will end today's service as we always do. Bow your head, close your eyes, and open your ears, A'Stavi!"

The Joebani people followed their High Priest's command and responded, "Gilaheed!" Though the chant was muffled by the kink in their necks.

"During the time of the Primordial Trinity, an era before the Gods,"

"All the water of Garsuna was trapped in the sky."

"When Apena (Maker of the Sky) used one of its three suns to shape Ruo, the first Goddess,"

"The sky mourned the loss of its kin, and for years, it cried."

"When Apena had emptied all of its tears, the skies cleared,"

"And the remaining two suns went to work reclaiming what was once in their domain."

"But do not fret and do not fear,"

"For Apena never forgets and will always relive the pain of its loss."

"And send its tears once more to Garsuna."

"A'Stavi." The High Priest concluded.

"Gilaheed!" The Temple burst into applause, the Joebani now eager to enjoy their day of Garsuna's Rest.

"Those of you who require a blessing, wait by the stage with your parents. Everyone else, may the Gods be with you." The High Priest of Joebanya staggered off the stage, clearly drained, and disappeared into one of the Temple's several side rooms. The lesser priests stayed on the stage, and the two Isonian Delegates took the High Priest's spot.

Not wanting to go against the flow of the crowd as the Joebani exited the Temple, Jason leaned back against the wall. As the crowd thinned, he observed the line that had formed along the stage. There were five mothers who held their newborns, a mixture of joy and anxiety painted on their faces as they imagined their child's future. Behind them were three young adults the same age as Jason, two with their fathers and the other with both parents. With the rate of mortality from childbirth, it was a rare thing to have a mother as an adult in Glotpon because there weren't any of Xle's (Goddess of Health) God Tools on the island. Jason made his way to the back of the line, the only child not chaperoned.

Jason almost half expected his adopted mom, his aunt, to meet him there. After all, she should've been at the Temple like everyone else. But as the line dwindled, she was nowhere to be seen. "She would've if she could've," Jason told himself. "Dad probably just won't let her…" Then, one of the teenagers in front of Jason let out a blood-curdling scream. His heart began to race as he realized he had no clue what was about to happen.

"Next," the two purple-eyed Isonians called out flatly. Jason stepped forward to the front of the stage.

The Delegates had removed their leather satchels and placed them on the edge of the stage. They sat at the height of Jason's waist, and he noticed both the satchels' flaps were only loosely closed. The Isonian Delegates stood on their knees behind the satchels, making it so Jason had to slightly lift his head to meet their eyes.

"Where are your parents?"

"They didn't want to wait in line," Jason lied.

The Isonians laughed for a short while, but when they noticed Jason wasn't laughing with them, they exchanged looks of amusement with one another. "It's better if we know which of Joeb's God Tools you were blessed with at birth, but that's fine. Just put your dominant hand into the right satchel, please, and don't look inside."

Jason peered down at the perfectly smooth satchel. There wasn't a single bulge in its square form, making it hard to imagine what might be inside. Jason gulped and slowly reached forward with his left hand. His body tensed as he imagined getting bit by some foul creature as soon as his hand slipped inside.

"WAIT!" one of the Isonians exclaimed, startling Jason. "My right, sorry. Your left."

Still confused about the whole ordeal, Jason went for the opposite satchel. His hand fell on a cold object that was undoubtedly refined iron. Jason tried to move his fingers along the object to get a better idea as to what it was. But then suddenly, everything around Jason completely vanished, and he found himself standing in a barren, black void. Even the satchel and whatever it contained were now gone.

"I remember you, child." The deep voice was more a presence than a sound, washing away any unease Jason had about being swept into eternal darkness. "Before the return of Chosrgel, we Gods and Goddesses delivered our blessings to all of the Descendants. But you've been the only one with Isonian blood to receive my blessing for a long time." Jason was about to close himself off, the way he always did when he heard those kinds of words. "Well, a long time for a human, that is, haha. But don't worry, Jason, I love you just the same."

"You... love me?"

A figure began to materialize several feet in front of Jason that oddly resembled the gilded statue of Joeb. Stripped naked save only a Victor's Sash with a perfect male physique. Chiseled body, chiseled face, and short brown hair. The figure's mouth moved, but Jason still felt the voice rather than heard it. "What kind of God would I be if I didn't?"

Jason suddenly realized that this was Joeb, the real Joeb, Craftsman of the Gods. "You're real..."

Joeb laughed, and Jason felt his heart flutter. "Where did you think you got the ability to manipulate stone, smelt metal, and create tools with your hands?" Jason shrugged. "Well, there's a reason we do this second blessing when you become an adult. One, it would be irresponsible to give toddlers the full breadth of power we Gods can offer a human. Two, you're at a skeptical part of life and we don't want you to lose faith, as that is the source of your power. And three, this is your only opportunity to truly ask a God for guidance. Well, the only time you'll receive a response, at least." Joeb looked at Jason with raised eyebrows.

"This is all happening too quickly," Jason thought. "I wish someone had told me beforehand..."

"It's okay, Jason, we have plenty of time," Jason nearly jumped.

Too scared of what the God might hear in his thoughts, Jason blurted out, "how do I get people to like me?"

Joeb smiled and replied lightly. "Why does everyone ask me that? At least it's an easy one to answer. Work for what you want, never try to be something you're not and surround yourself with people you love. Then you'll discover everyone in your life likes you. But always remember, not everyone is GOING to like you. Just look at the differences of opinion between Ruzar Ruzim and Gilstavi Gilaheed, and you'll understand what I mean."

Jason shyly nodded before asking, "how do I get better at using your blessing?"

"It will come much easier to you once we are done here today. Besides that, the only way to get good at anything is to practice."

"Practice," Jason wistfully repeated, as if he hadn't thought of it before.

Several moments of silence passed before Joeb said, "if you're satisfied, then all we have to do is make contact. Handshake, fist bump, hug, that kinda thing, and I'll bless you with my full power. Afterward, you'll be sent back to your body." Joeb extended a seven-fingered fist, which Jason was thankful for. He couldn't imagine hugging a naked man he's just met, let alone a naked God. After a moment of hesitation, Jason punched the God's fist.

The world suddenly materialized around Jason, his hand still buried in the leather satchel. He immediately noticed one of the Delegates had placed their palm on his forehead, a purple glow coming from their closed eyes. Jason pulled away from both the Isonian and the covered satchel and darted out of the Temple.

Jason clung desperately to the memory of his encounter with the Craftsman of the Gods. But for some reason, he could only recall one thing. A grimace that had formed over Joeb's charming face just as their fists connected. The God's demeanor went from inviting to discernibly deadly in a fraction of a second. Had Jason done something to offend the God?

CHAPTER 7
Catrina

Because the wet season was comparatively shorter than usual, the citizens of Qentonium finished their harvests in record time. This gave Catrina almost a dozen days to prepare for the coming Festival of Mahon. Catrina knew her spot was reserved amongst the ten participants chosen by the Council of Qentonium, as her father had already paid for it.

"Hey, Kick, wait!" Catrina heard as she stepped out of the house and into the muggy morning air, thick with dust and pollen from the harvest. Catrina turned to find Carey, her sibling closest in age.

Carey joined her older sister outside, and Catrina affectionately jostled her sister's hair. The teenager's face scrunched together as if she just smelt something foul, and she pulled away with both hands, clenching her blonde head. "Don't do that!" She whined.

"What's up?" Catrina inquired with a grin, playfully reaching above Carey's hair once more. The teenager squirmed from side-to-side, trying to avoid further dishevelment.

"I was wondering..." Carey dodged a descending hand. "I wanted to... Would you stop that?!" Catrina burst into laughter.

"Alright, alright."

"I wanted to ask if you'd help me... mmmm... get better with using my blessing?" Carey's face flushed, and she bent her waist into a slight bow.

"Of course," Catrina obliged, beckoning for Carey to follow. "Did father say something to you?" Catrina asked as she led her sister to the center of a barren field once filled with wheat. The topless stalks of the grass had already turned a dry yellow.

"He said now that I am an adult, I should get ready. Just in case..." The teenager walked through the field with her dress balled up in her hands. "Just in case he needs to send me to the Festival in the future."

Catrina let out a sigh of relief. Maybe Traxtione was actually serious about this being her last year. "Father knows what is best for the family," Catrina started to explain as she turned toward Carey. The poor girl looked so uncomfortably tense with her dress pulled to her mid-shin. "And if he says that keeping the Council's favor is what is best, then that is what's best."

Carey nodded delicately and defeatedly, "right."

Catrina clapped her hands. "Alright, kiddo, show me what you got."

Carey skeptically scanned the field of decapitated grasses, letting her dress fall to the floor as she relaxed her hands. The young woman took a deep breath and extended her arms ahead of herself, creating an upside-down L with her body. Her emerald eyes shimmered, and the half-dead grasses underneath her palms regained some of their natural color. Carey let out a long sigh; her arms fell to her sides, and her shoulders slumped.

"Great!" Catrina exclaimed. Truthfully, it was a pitiful display, but Catrina remembered being no better at Carey's age. The sisters didn't need to use their blessing on a daily basis to survive, unlike the average citizen. "Remember, it is the Gods who lend us their power. So, our strength comes from the faith that we put in them. It is beneficial to offer a prayer to Qentin before you try to use his borrowed blessing. Like this."

Catrina's knees fanned to either side as she crouched, placing her hands between her feet. She let her palms sink into the soil, feeling for the flimsy, shallow roots of the wheat. Catrina's eyes emitted emerald light as she recited one of the many prayers offered to Qentin. As she chanted, Catrina focused on the energy that circulated throughout her body. She visualized that energy flowing through her hands and into the soil, connecting herself with the wheat's roots.

Carey's mouth fell agape as she watched the tiny roots wrap around Catrina's fingers, crawling up her hand and stopping at her wrist. The stringy foliage had covered Catrina's hand like a glove, except where the stubbed end of her fingers should've been, the roots had formed sinister spikes several inches long. Catrina demonstrated her newly armored hand with one deft swipe, slicing harmlessly through the air.

"Now you try," Catrina invited with a smile. Her emerald eyes lost their glow, and the short roots blew off in the breeze.

"Qentin, Spreader of Seeds," Carey awkwardly started as she lifted her shaky hands. "Benevolent herder of the Trees, he who spared Foal, Goddess of the Hunt. I ask now that you see past my shortcomings as you saw past Foal's desires. See me for who I am, as you saw Foal for who she was. Please, Qentin Strong Bark, accept me as your own. For all I need is your guidance."

This time, the stalks of dying grasses underneath Carey's palms not only regained their color they also started to extend upwards. A satisfied smile spread across Carey's face, revealing her bright white teeth. Then, Carey's eyes fluttered, and she fell to the floor. A soft groan told Catrina that her sister would be just fine.

"Wonderful," Catrina said as she started to help Carey to her feet. "But you'd better learn to be careful. Our blessings give us the power to transfer the energy within our body into the environment. But unlike the Gods, the energy a human possesses is relatively limited." Carey nodded, too tired to do much else.

Catrina helped her sister get back to the house. The pair continued on like this until the End of the Month Service inevitably arrived. During the Service, Catrina, along with fourteen others, was chosen to represent Qentonium during the Festival of Mahon. The fifteen participants joined the Delegates on their way back to Isonia that same day.

CHAPTER 8
Jason

What Jason's mother told him was true. His abilities became much easier to control having received his second blessing. Afterward, Jason had a perfect sense of the flow his energy took as it moved throughout his body. So now, instead of building up that energy and releasing it in one burst, Jason could accurately supply consistent pulses to his hands. This created lighter combustions throughout the stone, meaning Jason could now bust rock apart without being a danger inside of a mine. Naturally, he returned to work as a Buster and several days later, Jason had enough silver saved up to rent a room. Though it was lonely, and at times, he missed his mother, Jason was proud of himself.

The month passed quickly, and Jason pretty much forgot that the Festival of Mahon was fast approaching. That is until the End of the Month Service. The Service started normally, with the High Priest of Joebanya recounting from The Record of The Faith. But before the High Priest dismissed the citizens, the Council of Joebanya and the two Isonian Delegates took the stage.

"The harvest in Qentonium was a success," one of the white-robed Councilmen declared. "King Akinish will send us our share of the rations any day now." It was one of the Isonian Delegates who spoke next.

"The Festival of Mahon will commence tomorrow at first sunrise and will continue for eleven days. Each day of the Festival will be celebrated to commemorate each of the eleven Gods and Goddesses. On the last day, to celebrate Cajo the Competitor, a special tournament will be held. This is a rare opportunity for those chosen to show their pride for their Province, as well as bring home an award. Whichever Province wins Cajo's tournament will be given the title 'Posebna' until the title is revoked at the start of the next Festival. The Posebna will receive the excess rations from this year's harvest as well as a special privilege in the following season's distribution."

Jason tapped his thumb on his thigh, a nervous behavior, as the Isonians' speech dragged on. He never paid much attention to this part of the Service, as the Festival of Mahon took place in Isonia. The only people from Joebanya who were able to go were the Councilmen, the family of the Councilmen, and the participants.

The Delegates concluded their presentation by explaining that fifteen adult citizens (those who have had their second blessing) who do not have a spouse will be chosen to compete in the tournament. The Councilmen picked their contestants first.

They chose ten participants, all from Crafter, Tinker, Minter, and Smith families, whose positions were paid for well in advance. The proud men and women stood from their seats and took a bow when they heard their name. Then, the Isonian Delegates picked the final five contestants.

Jason had a fleeting curiosity as to how the Isonians made their decision. He watched as they approached the edge of the stage and scanned the crowd. Every so often, a pulse of purple would burst out of the Delegates' eyes, and then they would call out a name in unison. Jason wondered if his father had a similar blessing and what it did exactly. Suddenly the Delegates locked eyes with Jason, where he stood leaning against the Temple's walls.

"Jason Miner," he heard it as a faint whisper at first, then louder from the front stage, "Jason Miner!"

Jason's jaw dropped, and he felt his heart in his mouth. "What?"

***

When the End of the Month Service concluded, the selected participants were instructed to meet with the Isonian Delegates. The two Isonians explained that the ride to Glotpon's capital would take the remainder of the day, and they hurried the Joebani into the now empty supply carriage. The vehicle was intended only to haul food, having brought the Joebani people their share of the harvest, and lacked any amenities one might expect on a road trip, such as seats.

The group was composed of four young women and eleven young men, ranging in age from fifteen to eighteen. Being one of the last to mount the carriage, Jason sat with his legs dangling out the back, shoulder to shoulder with two other participants. He recognized the two who shared the trailer seat. They were Natalia, she was one of the older participants and worked as a Prospector. The other was Alexi. He was Jason's age and worked as a Buster, though they weren't working in the same company currently.

The second sun had passed high noon when the Joebani were securely squeezed inside the supply carriage. The Isonian Delegates cursed under their breath at the Joebani for being too slow before grabbing the reins of their four bovine beasts that pulled the double-long carriage.

Jason had seen the carriage driving creatures before, known as brava, as they trollied the Isonians around Glotpon. Though, he had never been this close, and their sheer size was staggering. Appearing to be a mixture of oxen and horse, the brava were taller than a man by at least a head, as wide as three men, and had a pair of horns that haloed their face.

When the Isonian Delegates were ready, they didn't pull on their reins to get the brava moving. Instead, they recited a prayer to Isaa as their eyes manifested with purple radiance. Without concern for their cargo, the four beasts lurched forward, nearly dumping Jason and the two other Joebani out the back. Jason stabilized himself by grabbing the corner of the carriage, where the back wall intersected with a sidewall, while simultaneously thrusting his right arm to catch whoever sat next to him.

"Thanks..." it was Alexi who Jason caught.

"Don't mention it," Jason said. He kept his face forward, watching as Joebanya slowly shrunk. With every stride, the brava took Jason further and further from familiarity.

"Say, have you ever been to the Festival before?" Alexi's question was shaky, showing he shared the same nervousness as Jason.

Jason only shook his head. That would've been the end of their conversation, but then Natalia spoke up. "I have. This will be my second time." Alexi averted his dark brown eyes from his left, from Jason to his right, to Natalia.

"What is this tournament?" Alexi asked as some of the other participants behind the trio perked up to listen.

"If you ask me, it's a farce," Natalia stated bluntly with a grin. "It's supposed to distribute the power evenly amongst the House of Akinish and the rest of the Provinces. Except nowadays, it's really about who can give the crown the most gold." Natalia thrust a thumb behind her in an indicative gesture. "Just one of them paid more gold for their spot than you'll ever see in your life."

"So it's a gambling tournament?" Alexi asked. His dark brown hair was becoming rustled as he scratched his head.

"There will be gambling," Natalia replied with a slow nod, "but only on the Day of Tette. We're being sent in for the Day of Cajo, and that's really all I know. Every year, the competition is different. Or so they say."

"Cajo," Jason rattled his brain with a slight shudder. "Goddess of Shadows and War. Patron to travelers, warriors, and thieves alike."

Alexi gulped and whispered, "A'Stavi, Gilaheed," with closed eyes.

Natalia let out a light laugh. "Nothing to be too worried about. Death is strictly forbidden." Both Jason and Alexi let out a breath they didn't realize they'd been holding. "I'm Natalia, by the way," she said, craning her neck to look at the two boys.

"Alexi," who met the young woman with a terse nod, and Natalia moved her gaze to Jason, who kept his face forward.

"Jason…" he felt Alexi grow tense as he turned to face his two travel companions with a forced smile.

It was then that a heavy weight connected with the upper part of Jason's back, right between the shoulderblades. Someone shouted, "Bastard!" and Jason was thrown from the carriage. He tumbled to a stop at the base of the granite aqueduct the brava were following towards Isonia.

At first, Jason was dazed, with a faint ringing in his ears. Then, Jason was furious, and the ringing escalated until all he could hear was his own heartbeat.

Thump thump.

Jason got to his feet and stood as tall as possible as he watched the Delegates direct the brava into a wide u-turn. The Isonians chuckled as they approached and it looked like they were trying to say something, but not a word reached Jason. He walked towards the back of the double-long carriage to find someone had taken his seat.

Thump thump.

Jason heard himself from a distance, "which one of you pushed me?"

The young man who stole Jason's seat raised a hand nonchalantly. "Well, I kicked you. If that's what you meant?" Several others laughed from the back.

Thump thump.

Jason's body felt like a furnace, and a film of mist began to materialize around his body. The Joebani bully jumped off the carriage and started to square Jason up, a glint of hesitation in his brown eyes.

Thump thump.

"You don't have the gall," the teenager produced a weak smile as he slipped his hands into his pockets. "Everyone knows it's illegal to use your…" In a fit of blind rage, Jason launched himself at the bully.

First, Jason felt a searing pain on the soles of his feet. Second, Jason heard a loud pop as his shoulder connected with the young man's sternum. Third, Jason saw his world spinning violently as he and the other Joebani tumbled through the grass. And finally, Jason heard the faint sound of the Isonian Delegates yelling, "STOP! STOP!"

Chapter 9
King Akinish

King Akinish sat on his throne, the back of the gilded seat extending twice as tall as necessary. There were only two others present in the King's audience room, both of whom sat on less important-looking seats in the periphery of the room. They were the High Priest of Isonia, Casaba, and the King's Eldest son, Prince Akinish, who was at the age where he shadowed everything his Father did in preparation for his own rule. It was late, well past the second sunset, and the only light came from the braziers that were intermittently scattered across the King's audience room.

King Akinish was anxiously eyeing the entrance when he said. "Well, Casaba, this will probably be our last opportunity to prepare. I imagine that your responsibilities in the Festival will fill the next eleven days."

The High Priest bowed, "I appreciate your consideration, my King. If you would like, we can review all pertinent information."

King Akinish's eyes drifted from the door, and he removed his ornately jeweled crown, placing it in his lap. "That would be wonderful."

Casaba hid his reluctance and explained each day in depth;

Starting with the Day of Ruo, where the King would honor the Goddess of Life with sacrifices. This season, there were only animals to offer.

The Day of Sego, where the King honored the God of Thought with a day filled with competitive oratory.

The Day of Joeb, where the King honored the Craftsman of the Gods with the melting of the finest jewelry and idols. The raw material was then sent to Joebanya to be recreated.

The Day of Xle, where the King honored the Goddess of Health with a day of rest and cleansing.

The Day of Sab where the King honored the God of the Dead with the burial of the sacrifices made on the Day of Ruo, symbolizing their transition into Kigulbisis, the realm of the dead.

The Day of Hernic, where the King honored the Goddess of Weather by erecting a figure in her likeness composed of freshly pulled grasses. If the figure caught fire during the coming dry season, it indicated the next wet season to be short.

The Day of Tette, where the King honored the Goddess of Luck with a day of gambling.

The Day of Isaa, where the King honored the God of Water with the second day of rest and cleansing throughout the Festival of Mahon.

The Day of Qentin where the King honored the God of Plants with a sacrifice of crops relative to that season's harvest.

The Day of Foal, where the King honored the Goddess of the Hunt by releasing dozens of brava to be felled.

And finally, the Day of Cajo, where the King honored the Goddess of War with a battle between the four provinces.

Casaba lowered his voice and asked, "I trust that you remember what to do during the tournament of Cajo?"

King Akinish gave a dubious nod. "Are you sure there won't be any opposition?"

The High Priest chuckled. "You're the King of Isonia. Who else can oppose you? Once the word reaches the Provinces, though, it's only a matter of time until there's revolt."

King Akinish swallowed the fear that rose like a lump in his throat. "Are you sure a revolt is unavoidable?"

Casaba's lips curled at the corners. "That's the whole point of this stunt at the Festival of Mahon. Then we'll punitively purge the uprising, and your right to rule will be solidified not only by Isaa but by Cajo as well."

The King returned his crown to his head and gave a strong nod, more confident than before. Then, there was a loud rasping at the entrance of the audience room. All three occupants swiftly swiveled their heads and locked onto the door that was positioned directly across from King Akinish.

"Yes?" the King asked.

"It's Kennedict. I bring word of the Provinces' Participants."

"Please, come in."

King Akinish's Diplomat, the head of the Delegates, Kennedict, entered the audience room. Behind the Diplomat were two Isonians dressed in the formal, purple clothing of a Delegate. They both held onto opposite arms of a young man. The man's flaccid neck positioned his face to be parallel with the granite floor.

Kennedict and the two Delegates bowed before their King. Then the Diplomat announced, "all participants for the Day of Cajo have arrived in Isonia. Though I am afraid, there was an incident amongst the Joebani."

Prince Akinish laughed giddily, and his Father shot his son a chastising look. The King's voice reflected the frustration that should've been directed at the Prince, "what did this boy do?"

It was one of the Delegates who answered. "He used his blessing to harm another, my King."

King Akinish was hardly phased. "Fatally?"

"No, my King." The Delegate gave a cautious look to their partner. "But I do believe that was the intention. It was the most destructive demonstration of Joeb's blessing we've ever seen..." Casaba lifted a single eyebrow as he shifted to the edge of his seat.

King Akinish waved a hand submissively, his fingers swollen with jewels. "Awake," he uttered with a flash of purple from his eyes.

The young man steadily raised his head, and his eyes fluttered to reveal muddied, purple eyes. When he finally came to, he fought against the two Isonians who restrained him.

"Be calm, boy. Tell me what you did." The purple fire in King Akinish's eyes burned even brighter.

Unable to resist the King's absolute authority, the young Joebani stilled and started recounting what had happened. "One of the other participants pushed me out of the carriage whilst we traveled, and I took a hard fall. I just got so upset that everyone always felt the need to take their frustrations out on me. That's at least what mother always said they were doing... I wanted someone else to know how I felt for once. I didn't mean to use my blessing..." Jason kept his head held low.

The High Priest turned to the King with a start, but it was Akinish who spoke. "The law is clear: any who use their blessing to harm a fellow Descendant must stand trial for their actions." There was a light pitter-patter as Jason's eyes started to leak.

"Might I suggest mandating him to Temple Service? My King, that is where the Half-Bloods truly belong. He must be a bastard of one of the Isonian Delegates who got too lonely at a Joebani Service despite the decree." Casaba was nearly out of his seat.

The King looked at the High Priest with an empty expression. "Very well." Then the King yawned. "With the participants secured, I think it's time we all retired for the night. We have many long days ahead of us. Casaba, please show Jason Miner where he is to call home."

Casaba joined Kennedict and the two Delegates. The four Isonians copied Jason's composure and bent into a bow. The High Priest then relieved the Delegates and led Jason to the Temple of Isaa.

Chapter 10
Catrina

The first sun was setting when Isonia finally came into view. The granite aqueducts that spread Isaa's water throughout Glotpon looked like a spider's web as they shimmered in the sunlight. Catrina heard several of the younger participants catch their breath. Sadly for her, the spectacle of Glotpon's capital was lost on her the first time she saw Isonia.

The Isonian Delegates directed the brava and their double-long carriage to the stables. From the outskirts, Isonia looked like any other city in the Provinces. There were merchants bartering on every corner, and lesser priests were herding children through the decrepit neighborhoods. But as the Delegates took the participants further to the center of Isonia, it truly became the capital.

Merchants were no longer on corners but instead had their own storefronts. Citizens, rather than the lesser priests, tended to their own children. And the decrepit neighborhoods became lavish complexes, built tall and spacious. Just by walking down the main street, it was like entering a whole different world. The Delegates led the Qentonites to a circular building, which would've seemed tall if it hadn't been built across the street from King Akinish's Palace.

"This is the Stadium where the events of the Festival will take place," an Isonian Delegate announced as they passed through one of the building's many arched entrances. "You are expected to be present at each of the eleven events that honor the Gods and Goddesses. Some days will be more elaborate than others, but each day will commence at the second sunrise. If you fail to be present, you will be immediately disqualified from the tournament of Cajo."

The Delegate fell silent as they meandered around the curved hall of the Stadium. The building itself was more like a fence, which encircled an open field of sand. Before long, the participants had followed the Delegates down a flight of stairs, and they found themselves in a damp room carved into the Stadium's foundation. Apparently, they were the second of the three Provinces to arrive, as there were only fifteen other citizens present not wearing Delegates' robes.

"This is where you'll be staying," the Isonian Delegate grinned and gestured towards dozens of dingy-looking beds. "There will always be at least five Delegates present, so just try to relax. Privy is upstairs in the Stadium's main hall. Any questions?"

Catrina scanned the participants she hadn't arrived with to find they were from the Province of Hernicon, the blue-eyed fisherman. They were composed of six young women and nine young men. Catrina combed through the faces to see if there were any she remembered from the previous years. She didn't, but those Hernicon boys sure were handsome.

"When can we eat?" one of the Qentonites asked.

"Starting tomorrow, we will feed you three meals a day," the Delegate answered. "As far as today is concerned, that's not our responsibility." The young man who asked the question scoffed. "Anything else?"

"What are we here for?" another Qentonite asked.

"That will be explained on the Day of Cajo. None of the Delegates have been given that information either, so don't bother asking again. Anything else?" There was a tense silence, followed by the Delegate saying. "Alright, enjoy your stay at Isonia."

Catrina found an empty bed and sat with a sigh. The straw mattress was lumpy and carried a musty aroma, but it was much more comfortable than the carriage ride. Whether it was the bed or the noise of nervous teenagers, Catrina didn't find sleep easily.

***

The ten days leading up to the Day of Cajo moved at an excruciating pace. The participants were required to observe each day's festivities so that they could relay the grandeur observed at the capitol to their families back in the less important Provinces. The act was getting a little stale for Catrina, and all she could think was, "I waited another entire season to get married for THIS?" followed by a spiteful, "father knows best…"

When the Day of Cajo finally came, the Isonian Delegates woke the forty-four participants. Everybody was talking about the altercation amongst the Joebani, and the victim of the attack finally recovered and joined them several nights before. It wasn't uncommon for fights to break out in the transport to Isonia from the Provinces, but it was uncommon for blessings to be involved. Catrina half expected to see the perpetrator on the Day of Ruo as one of the sacrifices, but he was nowhere to be seen. Probably already executed for the barbarity or rotting in a cell.

The Isonian Delegates took the participants straight to the center of the Stadium. The hundreds of seats that cascaded down the Stadium's walls like a funnel were just beginning to fill. As Catrina's feet sank into the dry sand that composed the Stadium's Field, she was bombarded with a flurry of memories. The first came from last year when the competitors played a four-team capture of the flag. The second came from her first year, where she participated in a chaotic battle royale, fifteen v. fifteen v. fifteen v. fifteen.

Waiting in the center of the Stadium's Field stood the fifteen Isonian participants, King Akinish and Prince Akinish. The Isonians' pompous, lavender eyes hardly registered the arrival of the Qentonites, Joebani, and Hernikonians. That was until one of the Isonian Delegates announced their arrival.

King Akinish turned to reveal heavily bagged eyes. He then clapped his hands and said, "wonderful, right on time!" Prince Akinish mimicked the King but clapped with more fervor and joy on his face. "Without further delay, allow me to explain your roles in today's tournament. We still honor Cajo the Competitor, even though we have not seen war in many generations, because she represents an essential part of humanity. My Fathers believed that the peace on Glotpon has been maintained in part because we still honor the barbaric side of ourselves. So, in the name of peace, you will all be participating in a Single Elimination, three versus three, tournament. The winner is decided when they have successfully incapacitated all opponents or forced all opposing participants to admit defeat. As always, killing an opponent will result in your immediate disqualification. The home Province of the last team of three to win will be awarded Posebna!"

An uneasy chatter spread through the participants like a plague. The Festival of Mahon had been all fun and games up until now. It's different when you become the subject of entertainment rather than the one being entertained.

"Your Delegates have gone to the liberty of assembling your Province's five teams of three. Of course, the Joebani will have one team of two. Please meet with them. The first round of combat will start with the rising of the second sun."

Catrina obliged, noticing that the Stadium's seats were about halfway filled. The Isonian Delegates had put her on a team with two first-timers in an attempt to balance her exemplary experience. Both of Catrina's teammates were commoners. One of them even worked on her plantation.

"Benobi," Catrina said with a nod. "And you are?"

"Ilvia," the young woman answered amiably.

Catrina steeled her nerves as her father's words echoed in her mind, "...bring home victory for Qentonium... then I'll find you a suitable husband..."

"Alright, Benobi, Ilvia," Catrina beckoned for them to follow away from prying ears. "This is going to be our strategy..."

Chapter 11
Jason

Jason spent the eleven days of the Festival of Mahon confined to a small room in the basement of the Temple of Isaa. The High Priest of Isonia, Casaba, had said this was Jason's new home, but it felt more like a prison. The room was only large enough to fit two adults at a time, had one bed in the corner, and opposite the bed was a desk with a small stool. No windows, only stone that wept in the damp air of the wet season's final days. As part of Jason's punishment for assaulting another citizen using his blessing, his door remained locked until he was deemed safe by Casaba.

There was no way to know what time of day it was from within Jason's room without knowing the position of the two suns. He kept a tally of how many times he was fed in an effort to maintain some sort of structure. Between meals, Jason flipped through a copy of The Record that sat on his desk. Casaba said Jason would need to brush up on the teachings of The Faith. When Jason told the High Priest he couldn't read, Casaba said he would teach him later. For now, Jason just skimmed through the many elaborate depictions of the Gods.

The Record contained just as many paintings as words, allowing the large majority of illiterate Glotponians to understand The Faith. It showed everything; from the time of the Primordial Trinity, showing Chosrgel hiding in the shadows while it toyed with Apena and Garsuna, to the Fall of Mahon, after the Mother of Civilization brought modern society to the humans. Back then, there were some who deemed Mahon's use of the Gods' Blessing as blasphemous. The Record had everything in between as well, including several scenes from the Schism of Ruzar Ruzim and Gilstavi Gilaheed.

Jason had no idea how many times he had thumbed through The Record when the sound of rattling metal came from the other side of his door. Jason quickly closed the book and got to his feet. The lock fell to the floor with a dull thud, and the old hinges of Jason's wooden door whined in protest as it swung open, revealing the High Priest of Isonia.

Casaba slowly shuffled in, his age reflected in the abbreviation of his movements. The High Priest and Jason were just inches apart when Casaba closed the door. He then took a seat on Jason's bed, but the boy from Joebanya stayed on his feet.

"Is the Festival over?" Jason asked warily. Casaba turned to the young man to reveal his stormy gray eyes, and an inkling of suspicion sprouted in Jason like a seed.

"Not yet, m'boy. Today is the Day of Isaa, a time for rest and cleansing."

"Why are you here then?"

Casaba frowned, "I figured it was lonely down here." Jason scoffed but otherwise remained silent and vigilant. "Also, I figured that you deserved some kind of explanation. But just know this isn't how I intended for things to happen… Hm, where to start…." Casaba looked to the floor. "You weren't born in Joebanya, Jason." The young man crossed his arms. "You weren't even born in Glotpon, actually. You arrived with me almost sixteen years ago, from beyond the Enradic Sea. From a Province of Lamia, called Segocean."

"No, my mother died in delivery, and my father was an Isonian Delegate. My aunt and uncle raised me my entire life…"

Casaba smiled, showing the gaps in his teeth. "I never expected you to believe me, not initially, anyway. I just thought you should know why your life was spared," the High Priest started to stand on wobbly legs. "They're out there, you know, looking for you. And when destruction dawns on Glotpon, every bit of blood spilled will be for your namesake. After the conclusion of Mahon's Festival, we will begin your training. I just hope you harbor enough hate in your heart."

Casaba vacated his room, and Jason collapsed on his bed. "That old man has lost his mind," he thought to himself. "I know who I am, right?"

CHAPTER 12
Catrina

Catrina and her team had the second fight of the Day of Cajo, going against a team of Hernikonians. The blue-eyed fishermen with the ability to manipulate the winds. After the conclusion of the first fight, Catrina and her team hopped out of the Contestant's Box, a small area at the base of the Stadium's seats where all participants eagerly waited.

The three Qentonites walked to a ten-by-ten-foot square etched into the sand on one side of the Stadium's Field while the Hernikonians made their way to a different square on the opposite end. King Akinish was announcing the participants as Catrina finished deliberating with her teammates.

"Hernic's blessing is versatile. If they have any sense, they'll try to keep us off our feet. We'll need to remain rooted, and that in itself will consume a lot of energy. This needs to be quick if we want to win." Ilvia and Benobi nodded tersely. "Just keep them off me."

King Akinish finished his pageantry and then announced, "participants, Cajo is watching. A'Stavi!"

Catrina fell back as far as she could in the small square, and her teammates assumed positions in the opposite corners, creating a triangular formation. When they were ready, the Qentonites responded, "Gilaheed!"

After the Hernikonians voiced their equivocal assent, King Akinish declared, "BEGIN!"

Like flipping a switch, all six of the participants' eyes flickered brilliantly. The Hernikonians bolted from their square, creating a burst of sand. They moved so quickly that their movements appeared to be nothing more than a blur until they were positioned directly in front of the Qentonite's defensive triangle. The Hernikonians stood with their dominant arms outstretched, palms facing their opponents' feet, while their other hand stabilized their outstretched arm.

The roar of the crowd was dulled by what sounded like a deep breath, and that is when Catrina closed her eyes and started to recite a prayer to Qentin. Then, the three Hernikonians released their power, blasting the Qentonites with a gale-force wind. Just as Catrina predicted, they angled their blast at the floor in an attempt to separate their feet from the ground. Instead, all they sent flying was the sand, which scraped abrasively against Catrina's exposed skin.

When the Hernikonians realized their attempt failed, they moved with the same blurred speed back to their side of the field. Catrina finished her prayer just in time, and she slammed both fists into the shifted sand.

"Relax," Catrina ordered Ilvia and Benobi as she loosened the roots around her own feet. "Now it's our turn."

Ilvia and Benobi knew exactly what to do. They charged straight for the three Hernikonians as Catrina kept her crouching position, both hands in the warm sand. Not able to aid their speed with the winds, Ilvia and Benobi were far less fast than their opponents. But they still produced the desired effect. Their three opponents scattered in separate directions as Benobi and Ilvia neared, and Catrina's emerald eyes ignited.

The crowd gasped as a dozen vines, as thick as a man's arm, erupted from the sand. The vines chased after the three lightning-fast Hernikonians, and when the first one was finally caught, they retched out a surprised scream. The vine then dragged the young Hernikonian into the sand until nothing but a head poked out. After the last two Hernikonians were caught, Catrina's eyes lost their glow.

Akinish announced, "Qentonium takes the win!" and the crowd went wild.

Catrina waited for her two teammates before going back to the Contestor's Box, a wide grin on her face. "You guys did great," she exclaimed, offering both a high five.

Benobi returned the grin with a shrug, "it's just a matter of doing what you tell us."

There were eight matches to go before Catrina and her team were up again. Thankfully, they were on the left side of the bracket so if they won their next bracket, they'd be in the semifinals. Catrina used this time to analyze the contestants, and she instructed Benobi and Ilvia to do the same.

The Hernikonians always struck swiftly, relying on the speed and grace of their blessing. As Catrina demonstrated, as long as you can hold off their initial attack, they don't plan much after that. The Joebani relied on brute strength and their use of manipulating matter to create glass tools out of the sand. The Isonians did what the Isonians did best and used their divine right to rule to guide their opponents to defeat.

Ilvia looked to Catrina with a dumbfounded expression as a team of Isonians dominated a team of Joebani, "how are we supposed to fight that?"

Catrina smiled amusedly, "the Isonians' nomenclature is rather confusing, for they are not blessed by Isaa as most assume. From what I've gathered, they are likely blessed by Sego, giving them the ability to manipulate thoughts. Because of their over reliance on controlling others, they tend to think that we, too, are useless without our blessings."

Benobi watched in aghast as the Isonians used their blessing to turn the Joebani against one another. When only one hapless Joebani remained standing, the Isonians closed in on them. They resigned the fight before the Isonians were even within arms reach.

Benobi asked, "why didn't they just force their opponents to admit defeat?"

Catrina shrugged, "something about their sensibilities, I assume. They don't think Cajo would be pleased if they won their battles by just saying that they did." Catrina looked at her teammates with a sly smile. "That or they simply can't force someone to admit defeat."

"What is the plan, then?"

"Same as any other opponent," Catrina explained, holding her grin. "Beat them to a bloody pulp."

***

The next battle Catrina's team had was against a team of Joebani. Using a similar tactic to the Hernikonians, they pulled the win by overwhelming the Joebani with living vines. The semi-finals put Catrina's team against another group of Qentonites. Throughout the tournament, whenever two Provinces had a team pitted against each other, they opted to conserve energy by designating which team between the two had the best odds of moving forward.

The Qentonites that opposed Catrina said, "we'll concede. No doubt Companionless Catrina will win for Qentonium." She grimaced upon hearing the epithet given to her last year but otherwise agreed. And then Catrina, Ilvia, and Benobi moved to the finals.

Unsurprisingly, the other semi-final match was against two Isonian teams and ended much the same as the semi-final between the two Qentonite teams. That is without the name-calling, at least. By this time, the tournament had taken up most of the day, and King Akinish called for an intermission to commence until the setting of the first sun. When the first sun finally did set, the last two teams of three were called to the Stadium's Field. The Qentonite team found themselves in the same triangular formation, with Catrina in the back and Ilvia and Benobi in the front.

"Alright," Catrina started, "remember, withdraw from the fight right away." The two younger Qentonites gave a reluctant nod of agreement. "They'll only use you to get in my way…"

King Akinish asked the participants if they were ready with an "A'Stavi!"

The Qentonites and the Isonians replied with a "Gilaheed!"

"BEGIN!" and immediately, Ilvia and Benobi dropped to one knee.

With their right hands held high, they announced, "I forfeit!" By this time, Catrina was halfway across the Stadium's field, close enough to hear the Isonians curse under their breath as their pale purple eyes lost their shine. Catrina's eyes pulsed, and the middle Isonian's feet became wrapped up in roots. She leaped through the air and delivered a solid blow to the Isonian's jaw. They fell on their back with their knees awkwardly erect as their feet remained rooted.

"One down," Catrina thought as she turned just in time to duck below the two remaining Isonians' grasp. Catrina allowed the Isonians' assault to pull them to be positioned with their backs to her. She then interlocked both hands, raising them high above her head. Something stopped Catrina midway as she brought down her fists like a hammer. The Isonian spun around and, using their momentum, backhanded Catrina across the face, and she fell to her side, paralyzed.

The two Isonians blocked the light of the second sun, leaving Catrina in their shadow. When she finally regained control over her body, she stayed still. The Isonians inched closer, assuming victory, and in one quick motion, Catrina kicked both their legs out from underneath. She chose the closest one and jumped on top of them, straddling their waist to prevent them from fleeing.

Catrina was about to deliver a flurry of blows to the Isonian's face when King Akinish exclaimed, "STOP!" An odd hush fell over the crowd as one of Catrina's fists stopped just inches from her opponent's face. Catrina was once again paralyzed, but this time by a much stronger force.

There was the faint sound of shifting sands as King Akinish slowly made his way to the center of the Stadium's Field. When the King was in Catrina's sight, she saw that he held a Victor's Sash, the same one displayed across the bodies of the Gods' statues. Akinish draped Victor's Sash across his own shoulders.

"It is high time I resumed my natural place," King Akinish started to say softly. Then he raised his voice to a shout, "I declare House Akinish, Posebna for life!"

Chapter 13
Jason

Casaba came to Jason the day after the Day of Cajo. After that meeting, Jason's door was left unlocked, though he didn't venture out on his own for a while. The High Priest of Isaa would come to Jason's room from time to time, and true to his word, he slowly taught Jason how to decipher The Record.

When Jason had sufficient knowledge of the Faith, Casaba gave him the trademark orangish-brown robes of priesthood. The High Priest of Isonia offered to take Jason's old clothes, which were more old rags than anything, but he staunchly refused. Jason's adopted mother had made him these clothes for his fifteenth birthday, a symbol of his becoming a man. Jason would keep these rags underneath his priestly garb.

Jason slowly lowered his guard and spent more and more time outside of his closet-sized room. He met the other lesser priests of Isonia, and to his surprise, most shared his deformed, dark purple eyes. There were two others, Togashi and Semiel, that Jason got along with particularly well. And for the first time in Jason's life, he felt a part of a community.

Half a month had passed, and the dry season was beginning to show. The moist soil became dry and cracked, the days became shorter, and it was hardly bearable to be outside for even a few moments. During this time, Casaba hadn't said anything to Jason about what they spoke about the first night the High Priest came to the Joebani boy. And Jason hoped it stayed that way.

Jason was readying to retire for the night, and he knelt on the side of his bed with his elbows propped on the mattress, hands clasped together. Jason's eyes were closed, and he muttered a prayer under his breath;

"Hernic of the Wind, I ask you to deliver a message. Hernic of the Calm and of the Storm, please let my mother know I am doing well in the capital; she must be worried sick. Tell her that I have made some friends who are a lot like me and that I am safe. Oh, Hernic of the Breeze, carry my words through your winds and let her mind be at ease. A'Stavi, Gilaheed."

Jason sat in silence for several seconds when the unmistakable noise of screaming hinges forced him to look towards his door. As expected, it was Casaba who entered.

The High Priest of Isaa had a distant look and a faint smile on his face as if he were reminiscing of a time long past. "Come with me, m'boy," Casaba beckoned.

Jason obliged without so much a second of hesitation, his initial suspicion of the High Priest erased by sentimentality. Casaba and Jason walked outside of the Temple of Isaa and into the night. The two suns had been replaced by their less bright kin, the three moons. The largest of the moons sat in the background of the night sky, while the two smaller moons, less than half the size of the largest, sat in the foreground. The pale light allowed Casaba and Jason to see well enough to navigate to Isonia's Stadium.

To Jason's surprise, the city was as lively as ever. Fires danced outside of the large apartment complexes' windows, and the commotion of merriment reverberated off the granite walls. It resembled the exact opposite of nighttime in Joebanya.

"A time of turmoil is upon us," Casaba explained as the pair walked through the noisy streets. "The peace of Glotpon is dwindling."

"What do you mean?" A lump started to form in Jason's throat.

Casaba answered Jason's question with a question as they slipped through one of the many arched entrances of the Stadium. "What happened to the Gods in The Record after the return of Chosrgel?"

Jason hesitated as he rummaged through his brain. "It is said Chosrgel sealed the Gods within their own vessels, initiating an era of chaos. That was until Mahon discovered she could commune with the Gods by using their Tools that they were confined to. Mahon was the first to receive a blessing, and she brought society to humans by sharing this information with all of Garsuna."

Casaba nodded enthusiastically, "you learn quickly." Then his face turned grim, his stormy gray eyes nearly black. "There is a power in this world that seeks to possess all the known God Tools. Their reach is far, and their strength is vast. This power I speak of is the Segocean Empire, and I fear Chosrgel is the driving force behind their desires."

Jason shuddered, "the Record says the Creator of Chaos, Chosrgel, is always present. But why collect all of the Gods' Tools?" It was by this time that Casaba and Jason stood in the empty Stadium's Field, the signs of activity evident in the dents of the sand.

Casaba shook his head, "it's simple, really. The Segoceans wish to control the entirety of Garsuna, and they are willing to do whatever it takes. Chosrgel knows this and has shared with them a secret."

"A secret?" Jason's suspicions of Casaba resurfaced.

"Yes. The Segoceans somehow learned they could harness all of a God's power into a single individual. I don't know exactly how, but it results in the destruction of the God's Tool."

"How do you know all of this?"

"Because sixteen years ago, I fled the Segocean Empire with one of their weapons."

Jason thought Casaba was going to elaborate, but he didn't. After many moments of silence, Jason finally put it together, and his mouth fell agape. "You don't mean... me?"

Casaba's face hardened. "Yes, m'boy. I do mean you."

Jason shook his head, "no... No. My mom was Joebani, and my father was Isonian... Joeb even said he remembered blessing me during my infancy!"

"That may be true, but haven't you noticed that your blessing is a bit more... explosive than the other Joebani? And that you use your blessing unintentionally, almost as if it's second nature? That is because the Segoceans infused the power of Ruo's Reins into you, Jason."

Jason's mind was racing, "do I really know who I am?"

"Things are moving faster than anticipated, and I need you to be ready." Casaba's stormy gray eyes lit up like lightning. "We will practice here each night. Now, show me what you know." Jason nodded wearily.

CHAPTER 14
Catrina

The participants from the Provinces were allowed to rest underneath the Stadium for one more night before being sent home. Catrina kept to herself. Her fervor was replaced by devastation. The possibility of losing wasn't even on her radar, and she feared the consequences. She knew her father was desperate to claim responsibility for receiving Posebna to impress the Council.

When Catrina did arrive home, the families of the participants eagerly awaited their arrival inside the Temple of Qentin. There, Traxtione stood, looking like a bear of a man next to his delicate daughters, a smile smeared over his face. However, his smile turned into a quizzical frown when he noticed there wasn't a Victor's Sash present on any of the Qentonites.

"What happened?" Traxtione asked with a raised eyebrow.

Catrina recounted the events of the Festival of Mahon. She explained how King Akinish stopped the tournament of Cajo before it concluded and announced himself as "Posebna for life." Traxtione's complexion did not contort into contempt as Catrina was anticipating, but rather, he scratched the stubble on his chin.

"Take your sisters back to the farm. I must speak with the Council," Traxtione commanded. Catrina obliged and took her younger siblings home without saying a word.

***

When Catrina told her step mom about the events of the Festival, she took it well. So well, in fact, that she teased Catrina by saying. "Well, I guess it's another single season for you." Traxtione came home midway through lunch, and the chatter around the table diminished.

Traxtione took a seat with a contemplative expression. He filled his plate with vegetables and several pieces of fish before announcing, "Catrina, the Council is making preparations for you to be wed."

Catrina beamed, "thank you, father!" A weight was lifted from Catrina's shoulders. "Father does know best," she thought to herself. And then, "wait, why is the Council involved?"

"It wasn't your fault Qentonium wasn't elected Posebna, so I see no need to not stick to my word. The Councils have feared that the House of Akinish was growing greedier for some time now… You are to be wed to a Joebani, and as is the custom of old, you will be moved to Joebanya with them."

Catrina's excitement turned to inhibition. She had never heard of such a thing.

***

Catrina traveled with her father to the northern part of Glotpon on the back of a borrowed brava. The thick muscles of the beast were beginning to bruise both of their bottoms when the Runicon Mountains came into view. The sheer mountains created three lone peaks that thrust into the sky like swords. The closer they got, the harder it was to see the top.

Joebanya was located underneath the middle peak at the base of the Runicon Mountains. Catrina's first impression was that Joebanya was awful. It smelt like smoke throughout the entire Province. Their people lived in holes in the ground, and there weren't any towering trees to hide from the suns. She knew she was going to miss her sisters and wished for anything to be back on her family farm.

"Father knows best," she kept telling herself, and each time, she believed herself less and less.

Traxtione led the brava to the stables in Joebanya, one of the few pieces of above-ground infrastructure besides the Great Furnace and the Temple of Joeb. He then removed an elegantly embroidered emerald dress from the leather pack on his back and handed it to Catrina.

"This was your grandmother's…" Traxtione said with a hint of guilt. "Your mother wore it at our wedding, and I think she'd want you to have it for yours."

Catrina snatched the dress and quickly pulled it over her day clothes. The color of the dress matched perfectly with Catrina's emerald eyes, and it fit so snugly that it felt like Catrina's mother was giving her a hug. "I love it," she said with a twirl.

Traxtione gave a terse nod, a look of both happiness and regret stained on his face. Catrina's father then led her to the Temple of Joeb on foot. There, they found the High Priest of Joebanya, evident by his black robes, a Joebani Councilman with his pristinely white robes, and two Joebani citizens. One of the Joebani wore a tidy, tan tunic, Catrina's husband-to-be, and another who was dressed much like Traxtione. Both fathers wore plain linens so as not to outdo either of the spouses on their day. All eyes followed Catrina when she entered.

Traxtione kept his voice low, only intending for his daughter to hear, "I know you don't yet understand why you're being sent to live in Joebanya." He looked at Catrina, and she could see the happiness had faded from his face, leaving only regret. "Please know I am only following the Council's orders."

"It's okay, Father," Catrina whispered. "I know you only do what is best for the family." Catrina's stomach was doing flips. After hearing herself say it out loud, she knew her faith in her own words had completely diminished. "You're only doing what is best for you," she thought. But this was no time to think of such things, and Catrina buried her emotions, replacing them with a joyful smile.

Truth be told, Catrina wasn't impressed with her husband at first glance. He was the same height as her and had shaggy, reddish-brown hair and dark brown eyes. There were also the early wrinkles forming around his eyes from spending too many hours squinting into a furnace. Overall, her first impression was very average.

The wedding itself was relatively quick. The High Priest of Joebanya started by reading several verses from The Record about Xle, Goddess of Health, Love, and Copulation. Then, the Fathers exchanged wedding gifts, only fueling Catrina's new found contempt. Finally, Catrina and her new husband, Lukice, read Xle's Vow from The Record. And just like that, Catrina was now a Joebani citizen.

Chapter 15
King Akinish

"You played your part impeccably, my Lord," Casaba said. "My sources tell me that Qentonium was the first to act." The High Priest of Isonia bowed before King Akinish, who sat on his excessively tall throne. The only other person in the audience room was the Prince. "They are preparing alliances with the other Provinces."

King Akinish rubbed his chin contemplatively. "I don't think we can take on all three at once…"

"No, my King," Casaba said, shaking his head. "It does not matter if all the Provinces are against us now. When you annihilate their attempt at rebellion, show them how powerful you are, then the Provinces will have no choice but to follow you."

Prince Akinish rubbed his hands together and giggled but was ignored.

"Right, they will only follow me if they fear me," King Akinish recounted what Casaba had taught him.

"Exactly, and their current plotting only goes to show that claiming absolute rule is not enough. You must demonstrate your authority."

"How are we going to decimate these rebels? You know that the Isonian's blessing from Sego only allows us to control the actions of those who can hear our voices. And normally, no more than two or three people at a time and only for a few moments."

Casaba grinned, "leave that to me, my King."

Prince Akinish nearly jumped out of his seat with excitement.

CHAPTER 16
Jason

Jason's days became highly structured over the next month. Each morning he met with the other lesser priests to study The Record, then Casaba would visit the Temple and deliver a Service. Unlike the End of the Month Services, attendance wasn't required of the citizens, but many Isonians still showed up, not having much else to do. After the daily Service, Jason met with his two friends, Semiel and Togashi, for lunch.

Jason, Semiel, and Togashi always sat together at one of the round tables in the Temple's Mess Hall. Though Jason had just met the two, he felt like the third part of a trio he should've been a part of his whole life. Today, Jason was the last to grab his food. He plopped down between his two friends.

Semiel pushed his glasses up his nose, amplifying the odd, dark purple color of his eyes. "Carrots and peas with a little sweet bread, again. I'm sure you're just dying to go back to Joebanya." He said sarcastically.

Jason grinned, "oh yeah. Can't wait to get back to salt with a side of fish three times a day." Both Semiel and Togashi laughed.

"It couldn't have been that bad," Togashi said. "The Temple there would've had vegetables, maybe even fruit."

"But I didn't work in the Temple," Jason reiterated. He had told them several times, but they both grew up associating half-bloods strictly as Isonian priests. "I was a Buster in the mines and a lousy one at that."

"Ah, that's right," Togashi lightly slapped himself on the forehead jovially. "Well, we're all glad to have you here, right Semiel?"

"Sooooo glad," Semiel rolled his eyes and Jason gave him a playful punch to the shoulder.

"I'm at least happy to be here," Jason grinned.

After lunch, the lesser priests were expected to tend to the Temple and any who may be inhabiting it. As Jason knew all too well, the Temple acted as a refuge for those without anywhere else to go. Though it was nothing Jason had ever been interested in, priesthood really suited him. When the second sun finally set, Jason would wait in his room for Casaba to fetch him. The familiar sound of his door's screaming hinges indicated it was time to train.

"Ready, m'boy?" Casaba asked, enthusiasm stricken on his face.

Jason met his smile with his own, "yes, teacher."

Jason followed Casaba to the Stadium like he did every night. When they reached the Stadium's field, Casaba's eyes would flicker, indicating he had somehow concealed the area from prying eyes and ears. Truthfully, Jason still wasn't sure what Casaba's blessing or blessings were. Jason knew he must have at least two because the first thing the High Priest trained Jason on was differentiating Joeb's and Ruo's blessings.

"Let's review everything you've learned so far," Casaba decided, positioning himself in the center of the field. "Show me Ruo's flame." The High Priest opened his arms as if he were preparing for an embrace.

Jason tersely nodded as he bent his knees to brace himself, his eyes beginning to emit a deep purple glow. He had learned that Ruo's flame came from the warm sensation that burned within his chest. Jason concentrated on building up that warmth as he outstretched his arms so that his palms faced Casaba. Jason released all of his stored energy in one burst.

With a flash of brilliant light that illuminated the Stadium's seats as if it were daytime, an explosion erupted from Jason's palm. The force was so great that Jason skidded backward in the sand until his back smacked into the retaining wall between the field and the seats. Casaba caught the blast, and just as quickly as it was produced, it dissipated.

Casaba grinned. "You grow stronger with each day, m'boy. Now show me the power of Joeb!" Joeb's blessing was different from Ruo's as it relied on transferring energy into a specific, external stimulus rather than Jason expelling his stored energy.

Jason found his initial position. Extending only one arm, he transferred the energy that circulated to his hand into the surrounding air. Jason's eyes flickered, and his hand ignited. Jason then forced that energy away from his body, sending it directly at Casaba. A streak of fire licked across the Stadium's field, and as soon as it touched Casaba's hand, it was extinguished.

"Wonderful," the High Priest of Isonia said, walking closer to Jason. "Now, replenish yourself," and Casaba extended his forearm.

This was an ability specific to Ruo's blessing, giving Jason the power to absorb energy from the living. Jason firmly grasped Casaba's arm and created a link between his own energy and the High Priest's. It was an odd sensation for Jason as he was able to feel the full breadth of Casaba's being. If Jason could describe his energy as a pool, then Casaba's was an ocean. Jason released his grasp.

"That will be enough for today," Casaba decided. "You are progressing well." The pair started to make their way back to the Temple in silence.

"Do I really come from the Segocean Empire?" Jason asked abruptly.

"Yes, m'boy," Casaba said with a tired smile.

"Then why do I have the eyes of a half-blooded Isonian?"

"In the Segocean Empire, the Descendants have been freed from the shackles of lineage for some time. Thus, eye color is not as indicative as it is here on Glotpon. Most individuals are a mixture of the original Descendants' blood lines."

That sounded like a dream to Jason. "Why would you leave such a place?"

Casaba laughed. "It may seem to be a paradise to you, where individuals aren't judged for their appearance. But every society has its issues. The Segoceans have become obsessed with progression, but progression towards what? For all their power, they remain ignorant of their own arrogance. No, the Segoceans have known nothing but growth for generations, and it is time they understood some opposition. Because without opposition, what is it that we work for?"

"So you came to prepare Glotpon to defend itself from the Segoceans?"

"Precisely, m'boy. And without you, the Glotponians will be virtually defenseless against their power."

Chapter 17
Catrina

Catrina's husband, Lukice, was quiet at first. But the more they spent time together, the more they both warmed up. Lukice worked as a foreman in his father's shop, supervising the production of silver and gold coins. The business of minting was always profitable, and admittedly, Catrina should've counted herself lucky for she entered into a family even more vastly wealthy than her own. But even though she had been waiting for this her entire adult life, Catrina couldn't help but feel that something was still missing.

While Lukice trained new workers and ensured that the skilled workers were staying on task, Catrina acted as the last line of quality control within the family shop. Nothing could leave without her approval. It was work Catrina could get used to, but she did miss having the opportunity to use her blessing. Then, abruptly, everything changed. Just as Catrina was getting the hang of visually identifying impurities in a pressed gold coin, the shop shifted from producing coins to producing swords.

The metal presses were replaced with whetstones, and the small, circular vats were replaced with long, rectangular ones. Catrina kept her position as the final check before the boxing of the weapons. She found that checking if a sword had the strength and sharpness to slice through a man was less satisfying than guaranteeing the wealthy weren't getting shorted with their coinage. It made Catrina feel as if she were the one responsible for any damage the weapon might cause.

It was the second End of the Month Service Catrina attended in Joebanya, and she was as eager as ever for it to end. Traxtione had reached out several days ago to plan a dinner for their next day off, and Catrina could hardly contain her excitement to see a familiar face. The growing contempt she had for her father had been overshadowed by homesickness for now.

The High Priest of Joebanya was reciting the final prayer of the Service;

"Cajo of the Obsidian Dagger, Cajo of the Shadows, and Cajo the Defender,"

"Protector of Peace, forgive your children, for we have sunken to the level of beasts,"

"Sego's gift of compromise has fallen on deaf ears, so we must be the offender,"

"We do not fight for glory. We do not fight for feats."

"Our way of life has been threatened; those who were friends are now foes,"

"So we plead Cajo, Queen of the Gods, teach us the way of war, teach us all you know,"

"A'Stavi,"

Catrina let out a sharp "Gilaheed," and then she turned to Lukice and grabbed his hand. "Come on!" And she giddily dragged her husband out of the Temple of Joeb all the way to their hole in the ground.

"You get the water boiling," Catrina ordered Lukice as she meandered through the elaborate tunnel system that was their home. She made her way to the furthest back room, where Lukice had allowed Catrina to have a garden.

"You got it," Lukice's response sounded like a whisper, muffled by the dirt walls.

A reminiscent smile spread over Catrina's face as she used her blessing to speed up the growth of several vegetables. When she had a variable collection of onions, potatoes, carrots, and tomatoes, she carried them to the kitchen, where she found her husband loading the firepit with wood.

Catrina went to work chopping the vegetables while Lukice went to the water tank, not too far from their house. When her husband returned, Catrina's father-in-law, Plinus, trailed in behind him. Plinus and Lukice were the embodiment of an apple not falling far from the tree, and if it weren't for the age gap, they could've been twins. Lukice put the pot on the firepit, and when the water started to simmer, Catrina filled it with vegetables and a chunk of super salty fish. It wasn't long until Traxtione made his appearance.

"Father!" Catrina exclaimed, running to hug him. Traxtione's face was grim, but it softened a little with his daughter's embrace.

"Good to see you, Kick," he said after a hard gulp. He let Catrina go and looked at Lukice and his father. "Plinus…"

Plinus stood to greet Traxtione with a bulky arm extended. Traxtione met Plinus with a firm handshake and then he sat next to his brother-in-law around the fire.

Catrina still stood by the doorway, and her gaze dropped to the floor when she saw Traxtione sit. She then walked over to the firepit and slowly stirred the stew.

"Hernicon is with us," Traxtione declared.

Plinus let out a deep sigh, "I thought the day would never come!" Traxtione nodded his assent. "How many able bodies do we have then?"

"Tette willing, we're looking at several hundred men and women. The Council of Qentonium has issued a sword to all adult citizens, but training them is posing a difficulty. The Isonian Delegates seem to know the revolution is on the move, and they've started searching all cargo going in and out of the Provinces."

"Do you have enough supplies?" Plinus asked flatly.

"Should, at any rate. Let's play it safe and keep any new weapons and armor here in Joebanya. We will assess the need for supplies after our initial assault."

Plinus nodded slowly, looking into the dancing flames of the fire. "With the help of the Joebani Council, we've been able to set up training regiments deep into the mines where the Delegates would never look. Just make sure your people have enough experience. A tool is nothing if you know not how to use it."

"Agreed." It was by this time that Catrina served her stew to Traxtione, Plinus, and Lukice. They accepted graciously and immediately returned to their deliberation, talking with mouths half full.

"If the Isonian Delegates are getting as nosey as you say, we need to act sooner rather than later. All it will take is one of us getting caught, and this will all be for naught." Plinus said, his demeanor growing visibly more anxious as the conversation continued.

Traxtione picked something out of his teeth before responding. "We just need to make sure we can protect ourselves against whatever retaliation that waits for us. If we do not pacify the Isonians with one deft move, it will have been a daft decision in the end. So, what are you proposing, Plinus?"

"We strike in no less than ten days. We Joebani will approach from the north, the Qentonites from the west, and the Hernikonians from the south. The only way we win this is with surprise. Once that element is lost then so are we."

Traxtione scratched his blonde head, "you're not wrong. I just wish we had more time…"

"So do all who are put into a precarious situation," Plinus added quickly. "Sego be damned, he steals our time when we need it most."

The room fell silent and Catrina took her face out of her stew bowl, eyeing the three men who sat on the opposite side of the fire. She hated the Isonians just as much as any other citizen in the Provinces, but was revolting really the right solution?

"Have we not tried to negotiate with King Akinish?" Traxtione, Plinus, and Lukice swiftly swiveled their heads to look at Catrina, surprise stained on their faces. "We shouldn't rush into…"

Plinus laughed, cutting Catrina off, "you do realize what the Isonians can do, don't you? You'll ask for clemency and walk away with an implanted idea that you are the problem. No, the Isonians don't negotiate, they rule."

Catrina nodded solemnly. She knew better than most what the Isonians could do with their blessing, having fought them in the Festival of Mahon. "Why is violence the only language these men understand?" She thought.

"Ten days it is," Traxtione said after a short silence. Catrina's father then stood to make his exit. He was so preoccupied that he forgot to bid farewell to his daughter.

CHAPTER 18
Jason

Jason started to see less and less of Casaba as his time as a lesser priest continued. It got to a point where the High Priest of Isonia even stopped coming by in the evenings to tutor Jason. He assumed this was because his training was progressing smoothly, and Casaba trusted he was ready to defend Glotpon when the time came.

Jason reveled in his routine and had done enough Services that he hardly needed to use The Record for reference. He felt that his faith in the Gods of Garsuna was as strong as ever, save one. Jason's relationship with Tette, Goddess of Luck, left something to be desired.

It was several days after the most recent End of the Month Service when Jason was assigned to restock the priests' water, a job that rotated each day. To help with carrying the water, the Temple gave the priests a push cart, as brava weren't allowed in city limits due to their immense size.

It is said that in the time before the return of Chosrgel, when the Gods were free from their vessels, Isaa blessed Isonia with several fresh water springs. So unlike Joebanya, where Jason retrieved the water from a tank, here he got it straight from the source. The second sun was just about to set when Jason got the push cart to the pool located a little west of Isonia's market district. There is a spring in King Akinish's courtyard, which was practically the Temple's courtyard as well, but this was strictly reserved for the House of Akinish.

Jason dunked the last of his three buckets into the bubbling spring, which was set within a retainer of large boulders so that the spring could pool. He held it under the surface and watched as the air pockets fizzled, indicating it was full. Jason hoisted the bucket with both hands to his chest and shuffled over to the cart. But the bucket never reached its destination.

There was a loud explosion from the north, followed by the crackling of toppled stone. Jason dropped to the floor, knocking over his push cart in the process. For a short time, he lay in a puddle of ice-cold water, dazed. Then it occurred to him, "the Segoceans are attacking! I need to find Casaba!"

Jason leaped to his feet, ignoring the second explosion and his water, and he ran east, back towards the Temple. To get there, he had to cut through the market square, which had devolved into a riot. Merchants and customers fled simultaneously, creating a bottleneck in the streets. Crammed together in one sweaty mass, the Isonian citizens were attacking friends and family, clawing for a sense of security.

By this point, the commotion of combat rang from all directions. The clinking of clashing swords, the rumbling of tumbling buildings, and the scared screams of anyone who got caught up in the chaos. Jason could see the top of the Temple, but at the pace, the mob was moving, it was still so far away. He needed to think quickly if he was going to get free of this compressed crowd.

Then he remembered one of Casaba's lessons. Without a second thought, Jason thrust a small burst of energy to his feet, propelling himself over the crowd. Then, as if running through the air, he continued to send small, alternating pulses to his feet. When Jason had cleared the crowd, much to the verbal distaste of the Isonians below, he made his descent. Still unable to gauge his momentum accurately, Jason made a pitiful landing and somersaulted to a stop.

Ignoring the scrapes and bumps, Jason found his feet and bolted the rest of the way. He burst into the dimly lit Temple, exclaiming, "High Priest Casaba!" No response.

Something felt off. From inside the Temple, Jason couldn't hear any of the rackets from the raid happening just outside. In fact, he couldn't hear anything.

"Hey!" Jason's voice created sharp echoes as he called out to the three lesser priests crouched in front of the statue of Isaa. Jason rushed toward his three brethren, and when he was nearly upon them, his feet splashed in a thick, warm puddle. The unmistakable, metallic scent of blood filled Jason's nose.

"Hey," Jason said a little more cautiously, placing a hand on one of the priest's shoulders. With just the slightest pressure, the priest rolled to their side with a splash. That is when Jason saw the clean cut across the priest's neck, right below the glint of their glasses.

Jason fell dizzily to his knees, and he heard someone yelling, "SEMIELE! SOMEONE HELP!" It took Jason a few moments to realize that the screams were coming from him. Jason scooted his body along the floor, through the blood, trying to distance himself as much as he could from the corpses. He sat there for a while, in the silence of the Temple, with his back against the stage and his head in his hands.

"Why is this happening," Jason thought as he gasped for breath, trying to fight the tightness in his chest. "Was I not ready to protect Glotpon?" Then, a strong hand clasped Jason's shoulder. In a split second, Jason sprung to his feet and snatched his assailant by the wrist. Jason's eyes flashed a brilliant purple, and then he saw who had grabbed him.

It was Casaba, a grim expression etched over his face. "They're all dead," he said simply, keeping his hand resting on Jason's shoulder.

"The Segoceans…"

"No, m'boy," Casaba shook his head. "This foe comes from much closer to home. It is the lesser Provinces who have invaded Isonia."

Jason's sadness and self-loathing churned into unadulterated hate. "It's always them," he thought, "… When will they ever stop taking from me…" Thump thump. Jason felt his heartbeat begin to elevate.

"That's it, m'boy," Casaba said with a flash of gray from his stormy eyes. "Now go, defend Isonia. Return to them all the hatred they've given you."

Thump thump.

Jason's eyes grew wide and wild, "yes, teacher." Casaba had done something to him, and Jason watched helplessly behind his own eyes as his body began to move on its own.

Jason made to exit the Temple of Isonia, his far-off stare creating an empty expression as if he were sleepwalking. Just as Jason was leaving, three green-eyed Qentonites ran through the threshold of the door. Without so much as blinking, Jason lifted a palm in their direction. With one blast, he obliterated the opposition and doubled the size of the Temple's entrance. Jason emerged from the resulting dust cloud, a stream of fire following the motion of his hands.

He looked from side to side with glowing purple eyes, his vision blurred by rage. Then Jason positioned his palms to face the floor, and the flames that flowed from his hands elongated. Jason's feet slowly rose off the dust covered floor until he was hovering over the lavish buildings of Isonia.

Jason flew throughout the city, using the sound of clamoring metal as his guide. He indiscriminately torched anything that moved. When Jason needed energy, he would lower himself to the surface and find an injured rebel. He drew a sick satisfaction from watching their skin shrivel and the color drain from their eyes as his strength was renewed. By the time the first sun rose, the only sound Jason could hear was the light crackling of fire as Isonia burned.

CHAPTER 19
King Akinish

It was a miracle that throughout the entire raid, Akinish's Palace didn't receive so much as a single scratch. The King awoke the next day at the rise of the first sun, completely oblivious that half his city lay under cinders and ash. King Akinish opened the ornate double doors of his bedroom and was met by two things: a waft of smoke and High Priest Casaba.

"As requested, my Lord, the revolt has been thwarted." Casaba started as the King coughed, waving a hand in front of his face. Casaba began to lead the confused King through his palace and into the smoldering streets. "Though I regret to inform you that the raiders were formidable, and much of Isonia has been destroyed in the process."

"Do we know which of the Provinces are most responsible? We will make an example…"

Casaba shook his head, "no, my King. You've shown the people that your rule is one to be feared. Dozens of good men and women have been sacrificed to that end… No, now is the time to show the people of Glotpon that though you may be malevolent to those who oppose you, you can be benevolent to those who honor you."

King Akinish nodded, "of course, teacher. What would you have me do?"

"Compromise," Casaba said, crossing his hands behind his back as the pair continued their walk through the smoldering streets. "If you continue to rule with fear and hate, you'll only breed contempt, and your son will have a similar situation to deal with later. Now is the time to show the Provinces you can understand their miserable, meek existences." King Akinish looked to Casaba with a raised eyebrow. "Redirect their fear and their hate. Tell the Provinces you have the man responsible for all this," Casaba waved a hand over the destroyed city. "And as long as they agree to your terms, this man will stand trial."

King Akinish nodded slowly. "Yes… that's brilliant… Then they'll honor me for exacting justice for the murder of their kin. Where will I find this brigand?"

Casaba's face relaxed into a pleased smirk, "your leadership skills grow with each day, m'boy. You'll find Jason Miner in the basement of the Temple of Isonia. Now, I trust you can handle this. I will be making my leave to fight on other fronts."

"You're leaving Glotpon?"

"Only temporarily. I am going to attempt to barter for peace with the Segocean Empire before they reach Glotpon. Once you have assured the Provinces' loyalty, fortify the East Coast. Get as many of your people ready for war as you can."

Chapter 20
Jason

Jason awoke in his cramped room, laying as sprawled as one could in a single bed. He got to his feet, examining his space skeptically. And that's when he heard the too-familiar sound of screaming hinges. Standing on the threshold of Jason's door was Togashi, a dumb grin on his face.

"Togashi..." Jason whispered as tears began to well in his eyes.

"You sick or something?" Togashi awkwardly averted his gaze and scratched his head, uncomfortable with how emotional Jason seemed.

"No, I'm just fine," Jason said before he threw his orangish-brown, priestly robes over his head.

"Well, come on then, Casaba won't be happy if you miss another Service."

Jason made to exit his room, and without waiting, Togashi turned to make his way upstairs. Jason was right on his heels, trying to keep up while also trying to comprehend what was going on. When the pair were on the main floor of the Temple, they found the other lesser priests bowing before the Statue of Isaa.

"Come on," Togashi whispered, "Semiele is holding our spots."

"Semiele..." Jason thought wistfully.

True to Togashi's word, there Semiele was, his forehead pressed to the wooden floorboards. When Togashi and Jason knelt beside their friend, Semiele turned his head slightly to greet them with a smile. He looked beautiful.

Jason could hardly contain himself, and a single tear streamed down his face. He excitedly slapped Semiele on the shoulder, and that's when it happened.

"Jason, stop!" Semiele screamed as his robes erupted into flames.

Jason watched helplessly, his mouth agape, as a fire of his making engulfed the entire Temple. "It's not my fault," Jason told himself, looking down at his trembling hands. "It's not my fault." Jason covered his ears with his hands, but it did little to dampen the dreaded sounds of his dying friends.

***

Jason awoke with a start, his body drenched in sweat. He clenched his eyes closed, trying to erase the invasive memories that molested his conscience. But every time Jason closed his eyes, one of his victims stared back at him. Not a single one of them died with dignity; all were consumed with fear by the end, and Jason wondered if there was ever such a thing as dying bravely.

It took Jason a while to gather his surroundings. He found that he was kneeling on damp stone, held up by chains at both wrists. Jason racked his brain to remember how he got here, but the only thing he could think of was when Casaba ordered him to defend Isonia. The High Priest had done something to control Jason, making him unable to do anything besides what he was ordered to do.

"Hey, hey, I think he's finally awake," Jason heard someone whisper. He scanned the room but couldn't make out much in the darkness. All Jason could see was that he was behind several round metal bars. Then, a torch was thrust into Jason's cell, causing him to squint in the sudden brightness.

"Get King Akinish!" The man with the torch demanded. As Jason's eyes adjusted, he could see that he was alone in a cell and that the man on the other side of the bars was Isonian, evident by his pale, purple eyes.

Jason kept silent while he assumedly waited for King Akinish, "what have I done…" he thought while his neck slumped sluggishly. "Cajo the Competitor, Cajo of the Obsidian Dagger, Cajo of the Shadowed Pendant, please hear my plea. I have made wrong your rules of war, and wish to repent. I have sent the souls of my kin to Kigulbisis, the realm of the dead, for nothing more than hate and revenge. Please, Cajo, Queen of the Gods, forgive my trespasses."

Jason remained in prayer, asking all the Gods to forgive him for such ugly acts of violence. What bothered Jason the most was that despite being able to stop himself, he remembered enjoying the carnage as it happened. He vowed then and there that he would never try to reciprocate his pain onto others ever again. Such acts only created a vicious cycle of more hate.

"Jason Miner?" King Akinish cleared his throat when it was evident Jason was too deep in his own thoughts to hear. "JASON MINER!" with that, Jason jolted upright.

"Yes, my King," Jason said softly, bowing his head once more.

"I am grateful for your keeping my city safe," King Akinish started, hesitating to get to the point. "But you took things too far."

"Yes, my Ki…"

"SILENCE! The way in which you mercilessly mutilated your own kin it's frankly appalling. This time, you WILL stand trial for using your blessing to harm others." There was an awkward silence while Jason anticipated the King to say more.

"I understand, my King. May I speak with High Priest Casaba?"

"I'm afraid Casaba has left Glotpon for the foreseeable future," Jason heard movement that indicated the King had pivoted to make his leave. "The Provinces will be sending their own Councilmen to preside over this trial. I'll call on you once everyone is prepared."

"Yes, my King." Jason's voice was hardly a whisper, but it didn't matter. King Akinish didn't stick around to hear his response anyways.

"May Kigulbisis find you quickly, Casaba," Jason thought. "This is all your fault."

Chapter 21
Catrina

The morning after Catrina's husband left for Isonia with the rest of the Joebani regiment, she woke feeling nauseous. She assumed it was from her nerves, as when Lukice returned from Isonia the next day, it only got worse. Her husband had returned with nasty burns all over his body, making it look like he was covered in bloody bark rather than skin.

Catrina had filled Lukice's wounds with an herbal paste from her garden and wrapped his body in thin linens to help the healing process. After several days of washing and replacing the linens, Lukice's condition hadn't improved at all. That is when Plinus, Catrina's father-in-law, came to her and Lukice's home. Plinus didn't bother to announce his arrival, and Catrina was more grateful to see him than surprised as he poked his head into her bedroom. She rushed over to give him a hug, and Plinus flinched as Catrina unintentionally brushed over his wounds.

"How is Lukice?" Plinus choked up a little as he asked.

"He is in Xle's hands now. But I think she will see him through this; his condition isn't getting any worse, at least...." Plinus tersely nodded as he took a seat at Lukice's feet. "What in the good name of Garsuna happened out there, Plinus?"

Plinus shook his head, "we never stood a chance, Catrina. Those damned Isonians, they knew exactly what we were planning. And the second we arrived, they released some daemon of Kigulbisis to do their dirty work," Plinus shuddered. "Fueled by hate, the beast destroyed anything in its path…" Plinus looked to the floor.

"What of… what of my father?" Catrina's voice was shaky, and she knew the answer before Plinus even uttered it.

"I'm sorry, Catrina, Traxtione is gone." Plinus looked just as hurt as Catrina felt. "You should know he died honorably. Many of us, myself included, would not have made it back if it weren't for his sacrifice…"

Catrina fell to the floor, unable to still her wobbly legs. "How could I have been so obtuse…" she thought as she began to cry. Plinus put an encouraging hand on Catrina's back. "Father was never looking after himself… Father DOES know best…"

"What's…next?" Catrina asked, regaining her composure.

Plinus suppressed his surprise, "King Akinish sent his Delegates to each of the three Provinces immediately after the raid. After much deliberation, the Councilmen agreed to be unified with Isonia to create a single Province ruled entirely by the House of Akinish. And it wasn't just Joebanya; Qentonium and Hernicon have also agreed to become one with Isonia. However, all three Provinces had the same condition. Only if they can bring justice to the monster that stole so many of our kin."

Catrina nodded solemnly, "that is good."

Plinus looked to Lukice and then back at Catrina. "The Council of Joebanya have asked that me and my family come with them to Isonia for the trial. I don't think Lukice is in any condition to travel… Would you like to accompany me? I think you'd…"

"Yes," Catrina said flatly, keeping her emerald eyes forward. She knew this would be her only opportunity to get closure on her father's death.

"Great, we leave at the second sunrise tomorrow. I'll have my wife come tend to Lukice in your absence."

***

When Catrina and Plinus got to Isonia, the second sun had already passed high noon. The city looked completely different than it did when Catrina was present only several months before, and the distinction between the outskirts of the city was no longer apparent. It all looked decrepit, besides Akinish's Palace.

Evidence of repair was rampant across the city. Pulley systems were set along the aqueducts, hauling chunks of granite to patch the damages. Brava moved all along the streets, carrying carriages filled with ash, debris, and bodies. It wouldn't be long until the great capital of Isonia was restored to its former glory, if not built even better.

Catrina followed the group of Joebani into King Akinish's Palace. They found the King sitting in his audience room on a throne with an excessively tall back support. Present in the audience room was Prince Akinish, who sat beside the King, the Councilmen from Hernicon, and the Councilmen from Joebanya.

"Great, we're all here," King Akinish said with a clap and an oddly happy smile. "Now, I am sure a lot of you are confused, if not upset, at what has transpired here at Isonia. I am going to be honest with you, so I expect the same in return. I claimed Posebna for the House of Akinish because Glotpon is under threat of invasion. So, why is it that you oppose me?" King Akinish looked around the room.

There was some mumbling and scoffing throughout the crowd, but then Plinus responded. "I speak for all those involved when I say the House of Akinish has taken their divine right to rule too far. The Qentonites supply Glotpon with fruits and vegetables, the Hernicons supply Glotpon with fish, and the Joebani craft the necessary tools and currency we need to thrive. What do the Isonians do?" Plinus's expression was stoic, and his reply inspired many gruffs of agreement.

King Akinish scowled at first, but then he pondered Plinus's words. "We distribute Glotpon's resources, supply order, and maintain peace."

Plinus responded quickly, "that gives you no right to steal all of our country's resources for yourself."

King Akinish pursed his lips, "I'm sorry that you disagree, but that gives me all the right. Now, we can do this in one of two ways. Either I decimate the Provinces and appoint my Delegates as your new Councilmen or the Provinces swear fealty to Isonia. Of course, as my Delegates informed you, if you swear your loyalty, then you have my word, and justice will be brought to the one who killed your kin."

There was much-hushed discussion as a satisfied smile spread over the King's face. One by one, the Councilmen of each Province professed their allegiance to the House of Akinish.

King Akinish stood and delivered a bow to the Province's Councilmen. "We will have a trial first thing in the morning," he declared. "And then, for the first time in generations, it is time for Glotpon to prepare for battle."

A small weight was lifted off Catrina's shoulders, and she knew the rest of it would be released as soon as her father was avenged.

Chapter 22
Jason

Jason was brought to King Akinish's audience room early in the morning. He kept his head low while two Isonians led him to kneel in front of the congregation of Councilmen, wounded soldiers, and average citizens. Jason's lips were cracked, his face sunken, and his skin dirty from spending the last few days chained to a wall. Whatever was coming for him, Jason knew he deserved it.

"I have brought the Provinces together for two reasons," King Akinish started. "We must settle our differences and become a unified nation so we can prepare to defend our beloved island." The King cleared his throat. "Jason Miner, of Joebanya. You are here to stand trial for the destructive use of your blessing. As is prescribed in Sego's Law, we will allow the accused to explain their side of events."

Jason raised his head to scan the crowd. He had never seen an assortment of so many different kinds of colored eyes. All of them were staring back at him with contempt. King Akinish cleared his throat, and his eyes flashed with pale purple light.

"I said speak, Jason Miner."

There were several gasps from the jury before Jason spoke, "I was retrieving water for the Temple of Isaa when the attack happened. I rushed back to the Temple but was too late to save anyone. All the lesser priests were dead before I could intervene. Then High Priest Casaba told me to defend Isonia..." Jason scanned the room one more time. "I am sorry for all of the death and destruction I have caused."

King Akinish scoffed, "if anyone has any questions for Jason," several members of the jury jumped out of their seats. "One at a time, please."

The first man who spoke up was burly, had reddish-brown hair, and hailed from Joebanya, as evident in his brown eyes. "I was there the night of the raid, and the blessing you used was not of Joeb. What are you blessed with?" There were many murmurs across the audience room.

Jason hesitated before answering, "High Priest Casaba told me I was blessed by Ruo." The room was filled with indistinct chatter.

The red-headed, burly man had another question, "you said Casaba told you to defend Isonia? Was this a direct order?"

"Yes, but the way he did it… I suspect Casaba is blessed by Sego. Once he gave me the order, that's all I could think about…"

The next person amongst the jury to speak was a bald man, also a Joebani, who wore the white robes of the Council. "Jason Miner, the half-blooded Joebani, I remember you well. How did you become blessed by Ruo? We do not possess a God Tool of that Goddess here on Glotpon."

"High Priest Casaba said he stole me from the Segocean Empire," King Akinish's face turned grim for a second before he regained his composure. "He called me, 'one of their weapons.'"

Most of the jury that stood was now seated, their questions answered. All but one. She was a Qentonite, based on her emerald eyes and blonde hair, and appeared to be only several years older than Jason. "You took my father from me. Who is to say how many families you destroyed in just one night…" Jason looked to the floor, trying to conceal his shame. "Look at me!" Jason met the woman's eyes with tears in his own. The young woman examined his face before she, too, broke down. "Do you know what its like to be left alone in this world, Jason?"

Jason kept his face forward, his eyes locked on the Qentonite woman, "yes, I do. I am sorry that you do too…" The woman sat back down and buried her face into the shoulder of the burly, red-headed man.

"If there is no one else who wishes to ask…" King Akinish started to say, then another man dressed in the Council's white robes stood. This time, a Councilman from Hernicon, the blue-eyed fisherman.

"Let me get this straight… You are claiming that High Priest Casaba brought you here as an infant from the Province of Segocean in Lamia. He said you were one of their 'weapons' and that he forced you to defend Isonia with force?"

"That is what he told me, yes. He said the Segoceans discovered a way to give a human the full power of a God at the cost of the God's Tool. Then Casaba instructed me to demonstrate all the hate the Provinces have shown me…"

"Well, do you? Do you hate the Provinces?"

Jason looked around the room, scanning all the eyes that remained glued to him. "Yes," he said softly. "At least, I thought I did. But I understand now that I just hate being ostracized…" For the first time, the eyes of the jury darted amongst themselves, and the Councilman from Hernicon took a seat.

"If that is all the questions for Jason Miner, the jury may discuss their verdict," King Akinish announced.

All the Councilmen, the wounded citizens, and any others in attendance from the Provinces turned to one another, and a lively debate was sparked in the audience room. Jason could overhear part of their deliberation; some were saying, "he's as much of a victim as anyone else!" or "we cannot let someone that dangerous walk free." After a while, the jury hushed, and the burly, red-headed Joebani man stood.

"If what Jason Miner says is true, then this young man is not to blame. We find that the true culprit is Casaba, High Priest of Isonia."

Jason's jaw dropped, he couldn't believe his ears,

King Akinish grinned almost as wide as Prince Akinish did. "You would condemn my High Priest? I'm afraid we will have to wait until he returns." The jury erupted in a cacophony of complaints. "SILENCE! I have fulfilled my end of the deal and have given you the chance for Sego's rightful justice. If you choose not to pursue such justice, that is not my fault."

The burly, redheaded man spoke, "there is no justice in killing a scared child. Besides, if what you say about the Segocean Empire is true, we may need this boy."

King Akinish scoffed and gestured for Jason to be released, "the conditions are the same. I expect the Council of each Province to send their most able men and women to the East Coast. We prepare to defend Glotpon immediately."

When Jason's restraints were removed, he fell to the floor. The red-haired Joebani rushed to Jason's side, the young Qentonite lady in his shadow.

The Joebani man leaned down and put one of Jason's arms around his shoulder. He then looked to the woman, "help me." The woman scoffed, then reluctantly went to Jason's other side and wrapped his arm around her shoulder.

"Thank you…" was all Jason could say.

CHAPTER 23
Casaba

Casaba made his way down the bustling streets with haste. Even though he had removed the black robes of the High Priest, several of the citizens he passed still looked at him with confused but familiar glares. It has been a long time since Casaba had stepped foot in the Segocean Empire.

The High Priest of Isonia continued through the city until he reached the center complex, where the Temple of Sego and the King's Palace were located. Casaba quickly turned into the King's Courtyard and was immediately blocked by a pair of descending halberds. "Damn," Casaba thought to himself, "the one thing I do not miss is the guards…"

"State your business, old man," one of the two Guards said. Both wore the standard garb of a Segocean Soldier, segmented iron armor, a helmet with cheek and nose covers, and leather boots. Over their chest, the guards wore the bright yellow tabard of the Segocean, with the symbol of Sego's hourglass embroidered in blue.

"I have urgent business with King Maelokise."

"Yeah, so does everyone else. If you don't have an appointment, I can't let you through."

Casaba's gray eyes flickered like lightning, "what's the punishment for withholding information regarding the God Tools these days? I'm sure the King of Segocean would love to hear of two Guards who kept that information from reaching his ears, wouldn't he?"

The Guards pulled their halberds and said in unison, "you may pass." Casaba shook his head as he walked into King Maelokise's Palace.

Unlike King Akinish's Palace, the Palace of Maelokise was abhorrently lavish. Murals of the Gods adorned every wall, painted by the finest artists in Garsuna. The floors were filled with rugs and animal pelts, everything from canine-type pelts to serpent-like skins. And from the ceilings, opulent, golden chandeliers kept the Palace lit day in and day out.

Casaba made his way through the luxurious halls and sumptuous galleries all the way to King Maelokise's audience room. The High Priest of Isonia didn't even bother knocking. He forced himself through the tall, double doors. King Maelokise sat on his throne in the middle of the audience room, his mouth agape. Then he recognized who had just barged in, and he shooed away the Councilmen who were present.

King Maelokise was middle-aged, his light brown hair peppered with grays. He had a small beard that came to a point at his chin, which complimented the sharpness of his high cheekbones. The King shared the pale purple eyes of Garsunan Nobility.

"Casaba," King Maelokise stood from his throne and straightened his royal red robes. "We all thought… we all thought you were dead."

"Hah, dead? No, Kigulbisis doesn't suit me." Casaba said with a grin as he approached the King and embraced him.

"Tell me everything."

"You'll find I have been rather productive as of late. I located one of Sego's God Tools, the 'One Crown.'"

King Maelokise's eyes lit up, "so that's where you've been. And what of its owners?"

Casaba shook his head, "the fool doesn't even know how to use it. The One Crown is located on a peaceful island the locals call Glotpon. Less than ten days' voyage south into the Enradic Sea."

"Will it be easily obtained?"

"You could conquer the entire island in a day. I think Glotpon will make a fine addition to the Segocean Empire."

King Maelokise grinned, "I'll summon my generals at once."

CHAPTER 24
Catrina

The trial concluded with the Provinces agreeing to supply two hundred citizens each month to the Eastern Coast. King Akinish had asked for more, but after much discussion, it was decided that any more and the Provinces wouldn't be able to provide enough provisions and gear for their newly armed force. Then, the Provinces left Isonia as quickly as they had arrived, not wanting to loiter any longer than necessary.

Plinus had decided he would take Jason Miner in until he was sent with the first of Joebanya's two hundred troops. It didn't occur to Catrina that what Plinus actually meant was Jason would be staying with her and Lukice until then.

"I already have a house full of children," Plinus explained.

"You can't be serious… he killed my father!" Catrina argued as she shot a glare at Jason from across the carriage. "He should be in a prison, not my home!"

Plinus shook his head, leaning towards Catrina and lowering his voice. "The boy didn't even know what he was doing, Kick. We all know what it's like being a puppet for the Isonians, so show him a little bit more sympathy."

"Don't patronize me. I know what the Isonians can do. And controlling someone to destroy an entire city with one word isn't even possible."

Plinus shrugged, and he leaned against the carriage's canopy with half-opened eyes, clearly too exhausted to continue debating. "You will do as I say if you want to keep my son as your husband. That boy may make the difference between freedom and servitude."

Catrina's eyes burned with frustration as she fought back a rebuttal. She remained silent for the rest of the way back to Joebanya

***

Catrina stared at Jason Miner from across the room with crossed arms as he inhaled a helping of fish and vegetables at HER table. "So, this is the daemon of Kigulbisis Plinus spoke of?" She thought with a mixture of contempt and confusion. For some reason, she imagined her father's killer to be much more menacing.

"Thank you for the food," Jason said as he put down an emptied bowl. It was the first thing the young man had said since the trial.

"Hmph," Catrina snatched the bowl off the table with vigor.

"What was he like?" Jason asked amiably. "Your father?"

"What does it matter to you?" Catrina turned to meet Jason's gaze.

Jason's face twisted with guilt, but he was determined. "I want to know what I stole from you."

Catrina's eyes glazed over, "you stole everything…"

Jason walked over to Catrina and bowed at her feet. "I will never be able to replace your father, but please, let me do what I can for you and your family."

Catrina only scoffed, and she left the boy groveling on the floor to tend to Lukice. To Catrina's surprise, Jason followed her into the bedroom. When Jason saw Catrina's husband's condition, his face hardened.

"What can I do to help?" Jason asked.

Catrina stared at the young man for a few moments before responding curtly, "get out!"

Jason bowed and left the room. Catrina's emotions got the better of her, and she collapsed to the floor, sobbing. She found her composure and began to slowly remove Lukice's bandages while reciting a prayer to Xle.

***

The next morning, Catrina awoke to find Jason had already fetched the morning's water and had it set over the firepit. Catrina sat with a sigh just as Jason returned to the main room, hauling several pieces of wood. He tossed them into the pit and ignited a fire with his hands.

Jason turned to Catrina and bowed, "good morning." He said, but she didn't respond. "I am going to go to the morning Service, is there anything else you need me to do before I make my leave?"

Catrina was planning on ignoring Jason, but he awkwardly held his bow in the silence that followed. She said, "no," just to get him to leave. When he finally left, Catrina went to her garden to retrieve both herbs for Lukice and vegetables for breakfast. Catrina spent the remainder of the morning gingerly replacing her husband's bandages.

She didn't want to admit it, but Lukice's condition was getting worse. Every day, his bandages revealed more blood and puss than the day before. Catrina fought back tears as her husband groaned. The application of the crushed herbs must have stung his festering wounds. That is when she heard Jason return from the Temple of Joeb. Catrina kept her focus on Lukice when she heard the young man shuffle into her bedroom. She didn't turn to him, but she knew he was bent in a bow.

"I have returned," Jason said. "I sent all my prayers for your husband…"

"Don't you dare, mut!" Catrina snapped, turning to show her face stricken with fear. "You did this to him, so don't think for a second that your prayers will absolve you of this sin…"

Jason had bent out of his bow, and his eyes drifted over to Lukice's uncovered body. If his condition phased Jason, he didn't show it. He then slowly made his way beside Catrina and grabbed one of Lukice's hands. "His energy is nearly all but spent…" Jason said as his eyes lit up the room in a purple glow.

"Don't touch him!" Catrina exclaimed, trying to push Jason from the room. But Jason stood strong, unwilling to budge.

Then Lukice began to cough, and his eyes fluttered, "Catrina?"

"There," Jason said as he stood shakily from the bedside. "I gave him enough… of my energy that he should have…" he coughed before finishing, "a fighting chance." Jason was out of breath when he turned to leave the room, bowing in the doorway before disappearing.

Catrina collapsed over her husband, clutching him as tightly as she dared.

***

True to his word, Jason did his best to help Catrina and Lukice while he was in Joebanya. Each morning he would retrieve their water and then help Catrina with changing Lukice's bandages. Catrina's husband was growing stronger, and she had Jason to thank for that. Slowly, her perspective of the young man changed from that of contempt to that of companionship.

Over the next several days, Catrina began to notice that her belly was beginning to form a distinguishable baby bump, and her recent bouts of nausea all made sense. She told Jason to keep it from Lukice because she wanted to wait until he was fully healed to break the news. Then the day finally came, at the next End of the Month Service, when Jason had to make his leave.

Catrina and Jason sat at the table, enjoying a lunch of boiled vegetables, when Catrina broke the silence, "I didn't think it would have been possible."

"Huh?" Jason's mouth was full.

"I hated you, no, I loathed you for what you did… but now, I think I've found it in my heart to forgive you," Catrina spat on the floor. "I can't believe those words just came out of my mouth."

Jason looked up at Catrina with wide eyes, "thank you… thank you so much. Foal herself would honor your forgiveness…" He placed a hand on one of Catrina's from across the table. "We humans are so quick to deliver hate because it is the easiest way to take our minds off our own sadness. But such a reprieve is only temporary, and from what I've seen, that hate will only begets more hate."

Catrina pulled her hand out from under Jason's, "read that in The Record, did you?" she asked with a blush.

Jason just looked down and smiled into his empty bowl, "something like that."

"I expect you will be back in Joebanya when you're relieved off the East Coast? You at least owe it to Lukice. He is going to miss your company."

Jason's smile faded, "and I shall miss his."

Chapter 25
Jason

The East Coast was nothing but a rocky shoreline when Jason and the first of the troops arrived. Over the first several days, the Joebani, who were skilled in masonry, worked on building a fortified barracks. The Qentonites worked on cultivating a barrier around the beach with mangroves and thick shrubbery. The Hernikonians, who arrived on their fishing boats, established patrols along the shoreline, keeping a keen eye on the Enradic Sea to the East. And the Isonians, well, they did what Isonians did best: barked orders.

Once the infrastructure of the East Coast was established, the Isonian Delegates began requiring the present troops to participate in training. Each morning, the troops would run along the beach, and then they would practice using the swords and shields provided by the Joebani. After sword training, they had lunch, and then the rest of the day, the troops focused on honing their blessings. Surprisingly, the Isonians assigned Jason to be the instructor for the Joebani.

Jason tried to teach the Joebani everything Casaba had taught him. First, he tried to show them how to produce fire by transferring their energy into the air until it ignited. He found that the individuals with just Joeb's blessing could not transfer enough energy to spark a flame. So, instead, they worked on manipulating the beach's stone, using it to create tools necessary for war, such as spikes, shivs, slings, and projectiles. The days continued on like this for several months, and at the end of each month, more troops would arrive, and the East Coast Barracks grew.

Jason was wrapping up one of his training sessions when a man with reddish-brown hair and a horribly scarred face approached him. "Jason?"

Jason had to do a double take, but then he knew exactly who it was, "Lukice!" The two men offered up their hands for a shake but then brought it in for a hug. "Gods, it's good to see you out of that bed. How's Catrina?"

"Aye, you're telling me. She's doing fine, but she gets bigger with each day," Lukice made a roundabout motion over his belly. "I hope to be home before the baby is due."

"I'm happy for you," Jason said with a smile. The pair walked in silence as they made their way to the barracks.

"No hard feelings, alright?" It was Lukice who broke the silence. "Catrina told me that without you, I would certainly have..."

Jason waved a hand in a dismissive gesture. "Thank you, Lukice..."

All of a sudden, there was a blaring noise coming from a hallowed brava's horn that rang out across the beach. Jason quickly pivoted towards the open waters. Along the horizon, there were three massive ships, all flying a golden flag with a blue hourglass. The Hernikonian fishing boats began to surround the mini fleet. Jason and Lukice helplessly watched as a dozen black tendrils shot out of one of the massive ships, skewering several of the Hernikonians and silencing their horns. The tendrils dissipated into an eerie, black smoke, dropping the lifeless Hernikonians into the sea.

"Go alert the others!" Jason shouted as he bolted towards the Enradic Sea.

As Jason got closer to the water, a black mass formed at the front of the three ships as if some sea creature lingered just beneath the water's surface. The mass then separated itself from the ships, moving towards the beach at an alarming rate. When the shadow reached the Qentonite's mangrove defenses, it rose out of the water and glided over the flooded forest. Jason drew his sword.

When the black mass reached the shoreline, its form elongated until it resembled the silhouette of a man. By the time the shadow reached the sands, it had completely transformed into a human. The man who walked out of the waters to greet Jason was shorter than average, and he wore a blue, open-chested coat that billowed behind him in the ocean's breeze. His eyes were as black as obsidian.

"Aunder of the Shadowed Pendant," he said with a grin, slipping his hands into his pockets. "I come on behalf of the Segocean Empire; who might you be?"

"Jason," he hesitated, tightening the grip on his sword's hilt. "Jason Miner."

Aunder frowned, "pity. I'm looking for King Akinish of the 'One Crown.'" In an instant, the Segocean man disappeared and reappeared behind Jason, holding a knife to his throat. Without a moment to think, Jason forced all of his energy to his feet, launching himself backward into his assailant. Jason heard a faint chuckle as he skidded to a halt along the rocky coast. From the corner of his eye, Jason saw a shadow skirt in his direction, and he positioned his sword vertically across his body.

Jason felt a strong force slam into his sword. Then, a dagger materialized from the shadows beneath him, followed by the man who wielded it. Aunder grinned at Jason, then averted his eyes to look past the young Joebani man towards the East Coast Barracks. "Looks like you win this one," he said as he disappeared back into the shadows.

"Jason!" Lukice shouted from behind, followed by the commotion of several boots beating the ground. Jason fell to his knees, planting his sword into the ground to stabilize himself. "What WAS that?"

"Be on your guard," Jason shakily said as he got to his feet. "They've brought wielders of Cajo's blessing." Several of Jason's backup gulped.

The three ships from the Segocean Empire made it as far as they could before running aground, and their crews began loading into smaller boats. Meanwhile, hundreds of Glotponian troops streamed out of the East Coast Barracks, forming lines of defense along the beach. One of the Isonians had directed the frontline Joebani, where Jason and Lukice were, to sling volley after volley of rocks toward the ships. But before the projectiles even reached their targets, a torrent would rise from the ocean, dropping the stones dead in the water.

For a while, the smaller boats that the Segoceans were boarding advanced until blocked by the mangrove barricade. Then, when enough had been accumulated, a large wave lifted the boats over the trees, launching them towards the Glotponians' frontline. Jason was the only one who could avoid the wall of water. His dark purple eyes shimmered, and he leaped into the air, propelling himself above the battlefield with a stream of fire from each palm.

Jason watched helplessly as the Segocean used Isaa's blessing to spread their wave to the very back of the Glotponian's defenses, grounding their small boats. When the Segoceans released their blessing, the water receded back towards the ocean, dragging any Glotponian that got caught into the mangroves. The Segoceans had effectively removed their opposition in just one attack.

Jason flew towards the fleet of Segoceans, positioning himself between them and the East Coast Barracks. He landed perfectly on his feet with one palm extended in the "stop" gesture while his other hand brandished his sword. "I must look pretty foolish," he thought as one hundred Segoceans stared back at him with amusement.

Jason cleared his throat, "I do not wish to harm any of you!" he was met by a roar of laughter. "So please, go back to where…"

Two arms materialized out of Jason's shadow and grabbed him by the wrists. Before he had any time to react, Jason's hands were twisted behind his back, his sword clamored to the floor, and Aunder pinned him to the ground. Jason struggled to free himself, but it was in vain.

"Ah ah ah," Aunder whispered in Jason's ear. "You must have never heard of the Segocean Empire, huh, boy? It matters little if you want to hurt us or not because we want to hurt you. We're going to destroy this little island paradise of yours." Jason began to feel his heartbeat elevate. "And when we're done," Aunder licked the side of Jason's face. "You Glotponians will come to serve the Segocean Empire." Thump thump.

An image of Lukice and Catrina flashed in Jason's mind, first as a happy couple and then as bloodied corpses, worn from being overworked. Thump thump. Something snapped in Jason, like a crack across a pane of glass, and a grin spread over his face. "Hate only begets more hate…" he told himself.

"Just kill him already, Aunder!" One of the Segoceans exclaimed.

"With ple…" Aunder made a choking noise as Jason began to siphon energy from his opponent's body. Aunder then made a quick escape, fading back into the shadows and leaving Jason unabated. Thump thump.

Jason got to his feet and looked towards the Segoceans like a wolf looks at sheep. "Oh, how I'm going to enjoy this…"

The Segoceans quickly surrounded Jason, sticking swords and spears in his face. Before their weapons hit their mark, Jason's entire body shimmered as he sent a burst of energy in all directions. The resulting explosion erased any Segoceans within a ten-foot radius and wounded many more. The remaining Segoceans skillfully slid into a phalanx formation, using their shields to create an impenetrable defense from all angles.

The Segoceans used Isaa's blessing to send water darts at Jason as they steadily retreated, but their attempts merely dissipated from the immense heat that radiated from Jason's body. Jason lifted a hand in their direction, ready to blow the rest of the Segoceans to bits. But as soon as the blast left his palm, a foot came out of Jason's shadow and kicked his arm, misdirecting the assault into the sky. Jason tried to grasp at Aunder's ankle, but his hand slipped right through the man's body.

"We'll be back…" Aunder whispered into Jason's ear.

A thick black shadow then enveloped the Segocean phalanx, pulling them into the ground. It skirted along the beach, through the ocean, and then back onto their large ships. But Jason wasn't done yet.

He darted over to one of the fallen Segoceans and drew on their energy to replenish his own. Then, he thrust himself into the air, over the ocean, and towards the three ships. Jason could see Aunder standing on the bow of the middle ship, a smug look on his face.

"Looks like I won this one too!" Jason exclaimed before demolishing all three ships with a single blast from his palms. Perhaps it was his imagination, but amidst the destruction, Jason could've sworn he saw a small shadow slip away from the boats and slither into the ocean.

CHAPTER 26
Jason

Luckily, the Segocean's wave assault wasn't terribly fatal. The Glotponians suffered minimal casualties as a result of drowning in the mangrove's net of roots. When Jason had finished off the three ships, he immediately went to help pull the remaining troops out of the ocean.

"Where is he?" Jason thought to himself as he pulled an unconscious body to the surface. "Nope," he thought when he saw that they weren't Lukice. Jason continued this way until there wasn't a single Glotponian left in the water. "WHERE IS HE?!"

Seeing that the threat had left, the Isonians started to stream out of the East Coast Barracks. They began taking stock of the injured and helped transport those who needed medical attention inside the Barracks, where the Qentonite medics would tend to them. Jason rushed over to the first Isonian he saw.

"Have you seen Lukice Minter of Joebanya?" he asked.

"Jason, the Living Flame." The Isonian ignored his question, and Jason flinched at his epithet that had been spreading amongst the troops ever since he went berserk in Isonia. "We owe you our lives for your bravery." The Isonian bowed, a gesture Jason easily delivers but has never received himself. The Isonian's lavender eyes lit up. "Go, tell King Akinish what happened here today."

Jason returned the bow, "it would be my honor." Unable to ignore an Isonian's command, Jason made for Isonia still anxious about Lukice.

***

Jason found King Akinish sitting on his tall throne in the Palace's audience room, eating from a basket of plump fruits. Prince Akinish and several Councilmen were present, debating the shipments of troops and provisions being sent to the East Coast. When they saw Jason enter, they hushed their conversation.

Jason bowed, "I bring word from the Eastern Coast, my King."

King Akinish smiled as red fruit juice ran down his chin, "good news, I hope, Living Flame?"

"Casaba's attempt in diplomacy must have failed, as the Segocean Empire sent three ships. We were able to hold them off…" a grin spread over King Akinish's face.

"I knew you'd pull through for us, Jason!"

Jason held his tongue, waiting for the King to finish. Then he said, "I fear they will return. I spoke with who I assumed was their leader, Aunder. He said they were looking for you and the One Crown."

King Akinish's smile turned to a scowl, and he reached up to remove his jeweled headpiece, "the 'One Crown,' huh?… It is said that Sego gave this to Isaa as a wedding gift... Jason, you will no longer leave my side. If what you say is true, then they will keep coming until they have what they want."

"Yes, my King," Jason said, deepening his bow.

"If they return with Aunder or even more blessed with Cajo, the East Coast is all but lost if I'm confined to the Palace." Jason kept his opinion to himself.

King Akinish looked to the present Councilmen. "We must double the troops we send to the East Coast. Training is paramount; I will not forfeit the land my forefathers have presided over for generations!"

Chapter 27
Casaba

Casaba had resumed his normal position within the Segocean Empire as King Maelokise's personal advisor, helping to mitigate the struggles of the ever-expanding empire. In the sixteen years he had been away, many things have changed. Mostly, the Segocean's rule had expanded across the entire continent of Lamia, bringing in an assortment of new cultural practices.

For example, with the annexation of Foalanna, the Segoceans acquired the Bow of Foal, giving them a more ample ability to domesticate livestock. This turned the farming economy on its head, where fewer and fewer citizens relied on hunting. Now, the Empire focused its resources on raising brava and other animals for meat.

Casaba was sitting in King Maelokise's audience room, next to the King, managing a request for a road to be built from Segocean to its newest addition, Kahetic. The Kahetici argued that the road would help bring Kahetic into the modern age, giving them ease of access to the surplus supplies available to the Segoceans. Casaba argued that a direct route would cost too much when there were already auxiliary roads that connected the two Provinces. He decided to deny their request, and he received King Maelokise's nod of assent.

The Kahetici left, and Casaba called for the next appointment to enter. The man who entered had his hands squeezed into his leather tights, holding back the flow of his open-chested, blue robe. Casaba knew who it was immediately.

"Aunder, you return so soon. I expect that Glotpon was conquered swiftly?"

Aunder scoffed and shook his head, "I'm afraid I am the only survivor."

King Maelokise quickly got to his feet, "what?! Tell me everything."

Aunder recounted the events of the invasion, finishing with a grin directed at Casaba. "It seems that some information was withheld from us. The child of Ruo's Reins has been found."

King Maelokise looked to Casaba with an aghast expression. "What game are you playing, old man?"

Casaba chuckled. "No games, my King. I simply assumed the Glotponians weren't capable of stealing a Child of the Tool so easily." King Maelokise raised one of his eyebrows as he steeled his expression. "No matter, just send another of your weapons with Aunder. Gods, send three more. There's only one of them in Glotpon."

"Nobody makes a fool of the Segocean," King Maelokise gritted his teeth. "Glotpon will be razed to the ground. But we'll need to be more strategic this time... Aunder, you are to retrieve Haddrie of Sab's Shield. The two of you are to infiltrate Glotpon and take the 'One Crown' by any means necessary. And I want the Child of Ruo's Reins returned to Segocean at once, alive. I expect the next time I see you, you'll be the bearer of better news..."

Aunder turned to leave the audience room. He removed one of his hands from his pockets, raising it in a farewell gesture as he slowly walked towards the exit. "Yes, my King." Before Aunder reached the tall double doors, he dissipated into a thin smoke, vanishing from Casaba's sight.

Chapter 28
Jason

Jason was tormented by the same dream each night. He ran through a city wrought with destruction. Flames, smoke, and ash billowed in the wind, carrying the smell of death. Jason was searching for someone, anyone that could be alive in the conflagration. But by the end, he always collapsed in his own exhaustion, his hunt unfruitful.

Jason awoke with a start in his new bed, located just outside of King Akinish's chambers. The King had the bed specifically constructed so that Jason was within a shout's distance when they slept. Jason just shook his head and tried to go back to sleep, but his mind was racing. "I don't want to be a weapon. I don't want to spread hate and sorrow." Then Jason would remember the joy he got from killing the Segoceans that threatened Glotpon, and the taste of bile filled his mouth.

Eventually, the King aroused and retrieved Jason. They attended the morning's Service at the Temple of Isaa without any incident. But on their walk back to Akinish's Palace, same as every day and with every opportunity he got, Jason tried to convince the King to send him back to the East Coast.

"My King," Jason hesitated, choosing his words carefully as the pair turned into the King's front courtyard. "Isonia is far enough inland that we will know of another assault before they reach the city…"

King Akinish dismissed Jason's plea with a wave of his hand. "I won't hear another word of it. Your King requires you to be by his side, and that is where you'll stay." The King let out an exasperated sigh. "You and I are a lot alike, you know?"

Jason raised an eyebrow. "My King?"

"We were both born into a role that we cannot escape. Except where I was given a crown and a kingdom, you were given the destructive power of the Sun God, Ruo." King Akinish laughed. "And now I must protect my ancestors' home, much like you do, whether either of us want to or not."

"I see."

"My father always warned me that this would happen, that the House of Akinish would run out of Tette's luck eventually. I just didn't want to believe it would happen in my time. Gods, I'm scared for my son and my sons' sons…" It was then that Jason and King Akinish walked into the Palace's courtyard.

"I would be more worried about yourself if I were you," an ominous voice echoed over the bubbling of Isaa's spring.

Jason brusquely brandished his sword, "King Akinish, get behind me, now!" Something about the voice seemed eerily familiar.

It was then that two figures materialized out of the shadows of King Akinish's Palace. This time, Aunder brought with him a tall, slender woman with short brown hair and dark red eyes. Strapped to the woman's back was a big bulwark shield, about the same height as she was. The two Segoceans descended on Jason just as King Akinish slipped behind his bodyguard.

"STOP!" Akinish shrieked, and both Aunder and the woman halted midstride.

Jason skillfully sent a blast in their direction, bleaching the courtyard in light. But just as quickly, the woman with the shield used Sab's blessing and raised a thick stone wall between the two opposing pairs. Before Jason had time to think, Aunder appeared behind King Akinish. The wet sound of metal splitting flesh filled Jason's ears, and he turned just in time to see a dagger puncture clean through Akinish's chest.

"King Akini…!" Jason started to shout, but Aunder shoved the King's limp corpse right at him while simultaneously yanking Akinish's crown from his head. In an attempt to dodge the King's body, Jason shuffled to his side. He didn't even notice that a pit had opened beside him, and he fell straight down into it with a thud. The woman then used Sab's blessing, and the walls of the pit closed in on Jason, encapsulating him in a suit of stone. Jason's body became stiff in the confinement, making it hard to breathe.

"This can't be happening," Jason thought as he sent a blast all around his body. "Not now, not now." Another blast. He didn't know it now, but the woman's blessing from Sab allowed her to keep the stone that encased Jason's body from being destroyed by anything besides her will.

"He'll tire himself out eventually," Jason heard the woman say.

"No way Maelokise can be upset with me now," Aunder said with a laugh. "Not only will I be delivering him the 'One Crown,' but also the missing Child of the Tool."

"You mean WE," the woman emphasized. "Now, take us back to Segocean. I've already wasted more time than I wanted with this."

"Yeah, yeah."

Jason sent out another blast of energy in vain when, suddenly, the darkness that surrounded him lit up in a flash of white light. Jason clenched his eyes, and he felt the stone coffin he was concealed in begin to move as if he were floating down a river. Somehow, Jason knew that Aunder had taken him into the shadows and was transporting him to the Segocean Empire.

***

Jason couldn't register how long he was trapped in the suite of stone, drifting through the light-soaked shadows. But eventually, his body came to a halt and Jason was returned to complete darkness.

"Aunder and Haddire, welcome back," Jason heard an all too familiar voice say.

"Casaba," he thought as his chest began to tighten. Thump thump.

"Yes, as bearers of better news," Aunder replied smugly. "Here is your 'One Crown,' and as a bonus, we also brought him." The stone sheet that covered Jason's face crumbled into dust, revealing the audience room around him. First, Jason saw who he assumed was the King, with purple eyes and dressed in red. Then he locked eyes with Casaba. Thump thump.

"Wonderful," Casaba said with a menacing smirk. "Aunder and Haddrie, you seem to be able to control this Child of the Tool easily enough. I'll be sending the three of you to the south to support our forces who push deeper into Stellrend against the Ruzim savages." Jason heard Haddrie scoff. "Once you've made a real soldier out of him, bring him back to me."

Thump thump.

CHAPTER 29
Casaba

Casaba was retiring to his bed chambers within King Maelokise's Palace after spending the morning at the Temple of Sego for the End of the Month Service. It was the first Service he attended while back in Segocean, and it was oddly disheartening to be in the audience and not the High Priest's shoes. Casaba let out a sigh as he opened his door. He knew those days were sadly behind him.

Casaba took several steps into the room when his door slammed behind him.

"Ah, King Maelokise." Casaba started with a smile, turning to see that the King of Segocean had adorned King Akinish's 'One Crown.' "Does His Majesty require my assistance so that I am not allowed my one day of reprieve?"

King Maelokise stood silent for a while, crossing his arms. "You never struck me as a traitor, Casaba." He said coolly.

"A traitor?" Casaba raised one of his wiry eyebrows.

"Your return was suspicious enough. But for the missing Child of the Tool to be at the very island you were on for all that time? It's a little too convenient, I'm afraid."

Casaba chuckled and raised both of his hands in a defensive gesture. "And if you're right?"

King Maelokise slammed his fist into the wall behind him. "You know, with the 'One Crown,' I can make you tell me everything. So just spill it already." Casaba just met the King with a wider smile. The tension in the air rose to a pinnacle when both of their eyes flickered. King Akinish's a brilliant purple, and Casaba's like a flash of lightning. "Speak, old man!"

"Did you really think that Sego's paltry power would have any effect on me?" Casaba cackled as King Akinish let out a sharp gasp. "No matter. If you really wanted to know, all you had to do was ask, m'boy." Casaba took a step closer to the King, who backed against the wall with nowhere else to go. "I stole the Child of the Tool from right under your nose. The fact that the 'One Crown' happened to be on the same island was mere coincidence."

"But… why?"

"But why indeed," Casaba seemed to forget King Maelokise and slowly walked to the window next to his bed, his hands clasped behind his back. "When you have lived as long as I have, King Maelokise, you learn a thing or two about humans. Their aptitude for love and understanding, the ease at which they would sacrifice their own existence to protect what they love. But what is it that compels one to defend their loved ones?"

"I don't know." King Maelokise was still taken aback that the 'One Crown' didn't give him absolute dominion over Casaba's mind.

"It's hate. Hatred for the very thing that would threaten what you love. But just because you can't have love in your heart without also having hate, that doesn't mean the opposite is true. When a human knows nothing but hatred, THAT is when they become nothing more than beasts."

"What does this have to do with the Child of the Tool?"

Casaba looked backward at King Maelokise. "Because when the very world you call home is under threat, that level of hatred, that level of barbarity, it becomes a necessary evil to defend EVERYTHING that is loved."

"What are you saying?" Casaba then knelt next to his bed and produced a small lockbox. He walked over to King Maelokise and displayed its contents. Inside was a piece of lustrous metal that glared back at the King, leaving a little triangle of light on his cheek.

"I found this nearly twenty years ago, laying auspiciously in a patch of burnt grass." King Maelokise looked absolutely dumbfounded. This confrontation was not playing out as he had expected. "This means that they are getting close."

"Who is getting close?"

Casaba's lips curled at the corners, creating a grin that sat somewhere between menacing and endearing. "My people." King Maelokise's confused expression evolved into a grimace of fear. "If that's all you wanted to know, I would appreciate it if I could get back to the day of Garsuna's Rest."

King Maelokise nodded solemnly, and then he left the old man, closing the door softly behind him as a cold sweat beaded along his back.

Chapter 30
Catrina

Catrina thought that things were getting bad when the news of King Akinish's death reached Joebanya. Everyone was skeptical about Prince Akinish having the maturity to take over Glotpon, and several Councilmen even toyed with the idea of electing a prime minister until the Prince was more prepared. However, it was agreed that continuing to supply the East Coast Barracks with troops, rations, and gear was of utmost importance.

That is, of course until the Segoceans returned. They overran the East Coast Barracks in a single day and were marching on Isonia by first sunset. The Councils of the four Provinces met with the general of the Segoceans to charter a peace agreement before more Glotponians senselessly lost their lives. That is when everything changed, but at least Lukice was able to return home in one piece.

As part of the peace treaty, Prince Akinish took his father's seat on the throne but under the condition that his loyalty remained with the Segoceans. They then took all of Glotpon's Gods' Tools except two, one to provide Hernicon's Blessing and another to provide Qentin's Blessing. Glotponians were also required to join the Segocean Conscription when they received their second blessing. And finally, the Glotponians were required to give up twenty percent of all fish and crops to the Segocean Empire.

In return, the Segoceans provided several amenities, including roads throughout the island to make trade and travel easier, higher quality tools that made mining even easier, and better building methods so that no one had to live in holes anymore. As for Catrina and her family, Plinus had to relinquish his smithy, so Catrina and Lukice decided to move to Qentonium.

With so many of the Glotponians being displaced, Catrina's stepmother was able to keep the plantation, and she accepted Catrina and Lukice with open arms. Mostly because with Lukice in the house, it secured the odds the plantation would stay in their name even with the restructuring the Segoceans were doing.

Several months passed, and Catrina finally gave birth to a healthy baby boy. To Catrina's surprise, the boy's eyes were a light hazel color, almost golden in the sunlight. Lukice insisted that they named him Jason. Jason Planter.

Catrina was out with her son, letting him enjoy the cool early morning air before the rise of the second sun. She lay on her back, watching the thick clouds lazily scroll across the sky. Her baby was fast asleep, slumped across her belly. Catrina then saw what she assumed to be a bird approaching from above. She paid it no mind as it joined the clouds' slow procession.

The closer the bird got, the less it appeared to be a bird. It was completely circular and looked like a flattened stone, perfect for skipping across water. It produced a humming noise that was faint at first, but then the commotion engulfed all other sounds.

"What in Kigulbisis..." Catrina thought when her son awoke abruptly. "I need to get Plinus right now..." Catrina's baby began to scream as he pointed at the disc that loomed over his head. Catrina scooped him up and ran to her family's farm home. She turned to get one last look at the unidentified flying object. A tubular mass had extended from the bottom of the disc, connecting it with the ground. The tube was pushing aside massive mounds of soil as it bore a hole deep into Garsuna's surface.

Made in United States
Orlando, FL
30 June 2024